"Okay, Tara, demonstrate the next one."

Tara sent a nasty little "Try this, scud" smile to me before she raised her arms and rose into the air much faster than last time. She did a series of complicated spins and tucks, ending up on one of the steel beams of the gym, poised like a gymnast on the balance beam. She then dove off, head-first, went into a controlled spin, and pulled out just in time to land on the floor.

Coach Gertie seemed surprised. "My, my. You must think well of these girls, Tara, to give them such a difficult routine."

Tara looked like a picture of innocence. "Was that too difficult?"

Great. My first enemy and she's this year's head cheer-leader.

I thought I'd been smart, making sure I was at the end of the line. That way, I could scope out the mistakes other girls made and avoid them. Why was it that I kept forgetting my magic skills were at the remedial level? By the time it was my turn, my stomach was protesting the whole idea of doing a routine in midair. I ignored it. I wanted to make the squad. Strike that. I *needed* to make the squad, and chicken-ing out wasn't going to make it happen.

I raised my arms over my head and shot up faster than I ever had. . . .

Also by Kelly McClymer

Getting to Third Date

THE
Salem
Witch
Tryouts

KELLY McCLYMER

Simon Pulse
New York London Toronto Sydney

This book is a work of fiction. Any references to historical events, real people, or real locales are used fictitiously. Other names, characters, places, and incidents are the product of the author's imagination, and any resemblance to actual events or locales or persons, living or dead, is entirely coincidental.

SIMON PULSE
An imprint of Simon & Schuster Children's Publishing Division
1230 Avenue of the Americas, New York, NY 10020
Copyright © 2006 by Kelly McClymer
SIMON PULSE and colophon are registered trademarks of
Simon & Schuster, Inc.
Designed by Ann Zeak
The text of this book was set in Berthold Garamond.
Manufactured in the United States of America
First Simon Pulse edition October 2006
10 9 8 7 6 5 4 3 2
Library of Congress Control Number 2005937180
ISBN-13: 978-1-4169-1644-4
ISBN-10: 1-4169-1644-X

To Dad, who taught me everybody has a story.
You just have to listen. Thanks.

Acknowledgments
This book wouldn't be what it is now if not for the talent and
support of my agent, Nadia Cornier; my editor, Michelle Nagler;
and two women with expertly critical eyes: Beth Dunfey
and Kelly Moore. Their gentle prodding ensured that Pru's world
made it to the page in as much detail as could possibly
be tucked into these pages.

Chapter 1

Life is unfair. Mega unfair. And it's all my parents' fault. *I* certainly wouldn't choose to leave the house I was practically born in, not to mention all my friends, my school, my *world*. And just how sneaky was it to give me the cell phone I've been begging for since before I left for cheerleading camp (picture phone, text messaging, unlimited minutes, the works) just before dropping the bomb?

I should have known something was up. But, no. I was not prepared for them to spring the bad news—no, strike that. The *catastrophic* news.

We're moving. New state, new house, new school. No more sleepovers, no more a.m. gab fests with Maddie before school. No more . . . anything. Except, of course, magic.

That I can have. As if I want it. My life has been just fine without magic for almost sixteen years. So why do I need it now?

Mom and Dad are lucky that they have me for their daughter. Ten years of academic excellence and five years of cheerleading have taught me how to handle any crisis like Jane Bond—shaken, not stirred. Even when said crisis comes with a major twist.

I guess it's not surprising that, at almost four hundred years old, Mom thinks it's no big deal to uproot us. Witches think different, I learned that before I learned to walk. But Dad has no excuse. He's not even fifty yet, and he's mortal. He's attached to his things in a way witches outgrow around the hundredth birthday (or so says Mom when I ask why I can't have Dolce & Gabbana like the other kids).

I'd say my life is over, but I've used that line so often, it doesn't even get an eye roll from Dad. Would you believe Mom even did a little spell to make harp sounds play—just like she used to do back when I was thirteen and, I admit, a teensy-weensy bit of a whine-o-mat. And all I'd said, quite reasonably, was "I want to stay and live with Maddie until I graduate."

If only they were reasonable. But I guess I should know by now that *reasonable* is not one of the weapons in the parental arsenal.

Mom and Dad tried to softball the news that we were

moving from Beverly Hills, California, to Salem, Massachusetts, by telling us our new house had an indoor pool. Big whoop. Our old house had an outdoor pool, no snow in the forecast for a zillion years, and Beverly Hills High School, where I was going to be the very first junior to be named head cheerleader and maybe, just maybe, run for student council.

"You'll be running your new high school before long," Mom teased, as if she thought swapping schools was as easy as swapping Swatch bands.

Dad was more serious, as always. "As long as you keep your grades up, we'll be happy, Prudence honey. We don't need you to be head cheerleader or elected to class government to know you're special."

Special. He says that word with a wince. Poor Dad. He never really got used to living with a witch or raising two children who could do magic. If I were a good daughter, unselfish and properly thinking of my family, I'd appreciate how hard it was for him to agree to my mother's request to take us to Salem, her birthplace, so that we could learn to use the magic that had been highly discouraged here in the mortal realm.

Why did they suddenly decide to make this move? Did Dad get a fabulous new job at his advertising company so Mom and I could splurge on shopping and spa weekends? As if. No. We're moving because of Dorklock—otherwise known as my younger brother, Tobias. When the hormones hit, he couldn't control his magic. After the third time poor Miss Samsky's skirt flew up in the middle of summer school math class, my mother had our house up for sale and my golden life at Beverly Hills High up in flames. Boys are dumb. Especially when they're twelve. I would have voted to send him away to magic boarding school. But I don't get a vote. Because life is unfair.

I think Dad was tempted. After all, he is a non-magical mortal who is much happier when there are strict rules against uncontrolled magic in the house. But the idea that my brother could go to a school where teachers would be able to do simple spells against his simpleton magic until he learns to control it was a strong argument. Besides, my mother said she'd move us to Salem with Dad or without him. And he really adores her, no matter how much magic makes him nervous.

Dorklock doesn't even mind that he's ruined our lives. He thinks it's cool that we'll be in Salem, living in the witch realm and able to use our magic without the usual restrictions we have in order to live with mortals. What can I say? He's a kid. He doesn't understand that, as the newbies in school, we'll be on a lower scale than even the lowliest freshman. Of course, he's used to being a scud, the lowest of the low.

But I'm not. I'm honor society. I was going to be head

cheerleader. My life was supposed to be charmed, even with the big, bad magic prohibition. I had it all arranged—head cheerleader, and then maybe even class president. Fast-track ticket to the college of my choice in my pretty pink Coach bag. After all, I deserved it. I'd been working on being kewl since preschool. In Beverly Hills.

Thank goodness I know how to plan for the—majorly—unexpected. If I have to go (and apparently I do), I intend to keep my kewl. Even if I have to use magic to do it. Which is going to be a mondo change. Me, doing magic and not getting grounded for it.

But even I could not have prepared for just how fast our lives were about to change. The first thing that told me my life was going to do a midair flip in turbo speed was the actual day of departure. Instead of moving men and moving trucks, Mom flashed everything from our old house to our new house. One minute there, the next, gone. Dad kept watch at the window to make sure no nosy neighbors saw our insta-move.

Mom's sentimental and likes rituals, so we all stood in the living room and said farewell to the house. We sprinkled just a bit of incense to leave the next family a nice welcome, and then she said softly,

"Bless this house and all its walls,
We have lived here safe and sound.

Now we move to our new home,
Shift our things and cleanse this ground."

Zip zap. Empty rooms. Clean rooms. Fresh, blah cream paint on the walls. Even though the empty rooms of the house echoed and looked strange without all our furniture and knickknacks, I'd coped. But then I noticed that she hadn't just painted and cleaned with a zap.

"What happened to the lines on the door?" The careful nicks in the living room door frame that had charted my growth—and Dorklock's, of course—were gone. Missing. The wood was smooth, the paint perfect.

I'd been holding it together ever since Mom and Dad had said we were moving. No discussion. No appeals. No surprise. A cheerleader knows how to put a smile on, after all. But sometimes a girl's gotta let her true feelings be known so she doesn't get squashed flat like a frog on the freeway.

"The real estate agent will have an easier time selling the place if we leave it spiffed up," Dad said. "Wouldn't want someone new to have to do all the sanding and painting and such."

It was another sign that everything familiar was being turned upside down—Dad never calmly accepts Mom using "big" magic. Which is pretty much anything more than zapping an extra serving of popcorn if we run out and it's too late to run to the market. Normally I'd suspect him of taking a couple of Xanax, but he was about to drive and he doesn't even take an antihistamine if he's going to be behind the wheel. My dad makes a square look like it has sloppy corners.

"Put it back." I looked at Mom. "It's the house's character. You've said so a million times."

"It's only a thing, sweetheart. Remember, things are not important, people are. And the new people will make their own memories and create their own character for this house."

"It's not fair!" I whined. Harps sounded, mocking my words. *It's not fair.* I tried to shoot the thoughts through my blazing eyes. I think it worked, because my parents looked taken aback. And harp music didn't play.

"That's enough out of you, young lady," my dad said. The move had gotten on his nerves too. "Get out to the car right now."

I thought about making a grand gesture—running off to my room, slamming my door, refusing to go. But the room was empty. All my stuff was gone to the new house. Grand gestures shouldn't be wasted. We only get so many in one lifetime (or so says Grandmama, Queen of High Drama).

"Time to go." Mom was grimly cheerful. She was usually the optimist to his pessimist. But I think leaving was hard for her. This was her first home with my dad. Where she'd raised us. She was going back home, sort of. But I don't think she liked it. Not that she was going to do less than she thought was right for her children.

Too bad she didn't believe in witch boot camp. Dorklock was the perfect candidate. He was already out in the SUV, just waiting to go. He didn't even mind leaving everything behind. He'd like boot camp. It was the perfect solution. Apparently, in her eyes, perfect mothers didn't send their imperfect children away. Too bad she couldn't see the situation through my eyes.

Then again, maybe she did, a little. She put her arm around me and led me out. As we passed the door, she touched the spot where the notches had been and they reappeared. "Even a new family can enjoy a little lingering character."

"Just a minute." I stood there looking at the naked rooms that weren't anything like home anymore. I touched the top notch, and my name, PRUDENCE, appeared in the wood. Not to leave the Dorklock out, although he probably deserved it, I touched his top line and his name, TOBIAS, appeared. His top line was only a little under mine, despite the fact that he's four years younger. Soon he would be taller. Would there be a door frame to notch in the new house? And did it matter, when it wasn't home and never would be?

For a moment, I considered locking the front door to the house and refusing to leave. But, seriously, I'm in it to win it, just like a good cheerleader should be. What was there to win in refusing to go? An empty house that wasn't ours anymore? All my things were far away, in Salem.

Still, it was hard not to revert to the Terrible Twos. And I guess it showed, because when Dad came back he gave Mom that "Is she sane?" look they like to use when they think I'm being unreasonable. "Ready, princess?"

Princess? More like medieval serf. It's a wonder I'm a leader at school, considering how they treat me like a baby. I tried not to cry. Crying makes my voice shake. And voice-shaking is not leadership-quality behavior. I may have been forced to leave my cheerleading squad behind, but I would go with head high and a big fake smile in place. If only—

"We're going to come back," I began. "Why can't we just leave the house . . ."

"I'm not made of money, princess. We'll make a nice profit on the house. That's how we can afford the pool in the new place."

Pool. Big deal. Although, I suppose it could come in handy in establishing kewl status in Salem.

I walked out the door, fighting tears, to see a dozen girls in cheerleading uniforms on the lawn Tobias had just mowed for the last time this morning. The whole A squad.

All sixteen of them, including Chezzie, who hates me, and Maddie, my best friend. In full gear.

All I could think for a second was that I needed to grab my uniform and fall in line. But I'd turned my uniform in to Coach. In the heartbeat it took for the gut-punch to hit me that I was no longer a part of the squad, that it was complete without me, they geared up and began a cheer.

"Gimme a B!"

"Gimme a Y!"

"Gimme an E!"

"Noooooooooooooooooooooo."

"We love Pru so so much."

"We can't let her goooooo."

"So come back soon and we'll cheer."

"For Pru, our leader dear."

I didn't want to cry, because Chezzie was watching and she'd tell everyone, including Brent, my crush du jour. I'd been planning to wage a campaign to get him to take me to the junior prom this year. It was bad enough that I had to leave without knowing if the definite buzz between Brent and me would turn into a nice hot relationship. I didn't need Chezzie talking to him and making sure he wouldn't talk to me if I *did* manage to talk Mom and Dad into coming back. I could just imagine, "She was so jealous of how good we looked without her, she was screaming with rage." Chezzie puts the yotch in beeyotch.

Not that Chezzie would be wrong. I *was* jealous of them. Jealous that their worlds weren't being ripped into confetti. Jealous that they weren't going to have to piece all the confetti together again in another place and put on a smile while doing it.

So by the time the cheer ended, I'd managed to stop the waterworks. My cheeks were wet and I know my mascara was probably running, but at least I wasn't squirting tears like an insane teenage water fountain. I wish I'd thought to put on waterproof mascara, but I hadn't been planning to swim—or cry my eyes out either.

The squad stood for a moment in ready position, like we'd all been taught: take the bow, accept the appreciation, be proud. I had about a nanosecond to respond, and the wrong response could mean I'd be lower than a scud if I was lucky enough to convince my parents to come back home where we belonged. Reputation is precious, and I didn't want to lose mine in the last sixty seconds I lived in Beverly Hills.

"You guys!" I ran to hug them before they could move toward me. "I'm going to miss you!" I really was going to miss everyone but Chezzie, the snake with fake double-D's, but there was no point saying so out loud. Truth is, a good head cheerleader knows her team, and I knew mine, good and bad.

Maddie ran to meet me and we hugged. There were tears in her eyes and her embrace was no weak-armed "let me see whether you have silicone or saline" hug. She grabbed me like she wasn't going to let me go. Now I had an excuse for my drippy mascara. She whispered, "Run away and I'll sneak you into my closet. No one will know."

"My mom knows everything." It's a standing joke with my friends and enemies alike that my mother knows what I do before I do it. They don't know the half of it. Mom has those CIA tracking devices in the movies beat—she's set so many protective spells over me, it's amazing I can walk or talk half the time.

"I'll distract her. You run. 'Cause I don't think I can face junior year without you." That's Maddie, trying to cheer me up by letting me know how miserable she is. "You'll be fine. Look at what a great cheer you just gave." Besides, she wasn't changing schools and didn't have to snarf up kewl status from squat. But there was no point sour-graping her. It wasn't her fault I was moving. And she *had* offered me her closet.

"But you've been working on the cheer routine all summer. All we did was tweak it to fit today."

Trust Maddie to think that would make me feel better. I'd given her the notebook with all my routines and the music. Not that Maddie would ever be captain of the squad. She's a mouse when it comes to leadership. She's a great right hand, and I wish I could pack her in my suitcase, but I only gave her the notebook because I couldn't bear to give it to Chezzie.

I hugged her tight. "I'm going to miss you most of all. Don't forget to text me everything that's happening."

"You too." She glanced at my dad, who was making shooing motions toward the car. "Maybe you can come back soon."

"Maybe." I didn't try to sound hopeful. I wasn't.

"The team thought you should have this." Chezzie walked up to us and thrust a package with a big bow on it at me. "Salem—isn't that where the witches were? That should make you feel at home."

Chezzie and I used to be best friends. Until I told her I was a witch and she pulled out her cross and holy water and started to exorcise me. Picture me and Chezzie, about eight. She has a pink plastic bottle of holy water and a matching lavendar cross. I have a horrified expression.

Even though Mom wiped her memory, mine is still intact. Chezzie is prejudiced, and I'm just not up with that. Not that she remembers I'm a real witch, of course. But something stuck, because if she's not calling me a bitch, she's calling me a witch. It'll be interesting to see what witches call one another when they're PMSing. Mortals? I don't think so.

Chezzie was smiling and acting like she was joking, but I knew better. I unwrapped the package to find a shiny new Splitflex. Perfect for the girl without a cheer-leading squad. Still, I hugged her and laughed. "Good luck to all of you—and be good to your new captain, whoever she is."

That dimmed Chezzie's bleached-bright grin. But only for a second. "Oh, I'll make sure they are. And don't worry, I'll be a good captain, maybe even better than you would have been."

"Ouch," interjected Sarah, a strong girl who could hold and throw like a guy and had about as much sensitivity to girl-speak. "Is that your way of saying, 'Don't let the door hit you in the butt on your way out'?"

Maddie frowned at her. But after I had torn up my uniform and had to zap it back together to hand in to Coach, I had accepted that fate had spoken. I wasn't going to be the youngest head cheerleader of the Beverly Hills High School squad. It was a size-zero comfort that Chezzie was a senior, so she wouldn't be taking everything from me—just the work, the fun, and the glory. "Chezzie, I wish you all the votes you deserve, girl. And I look forward to seeing you in the finals."

She looked surprised. They all did. "You mean you'd be a cheerleader on another school's squad?"

Truth time? The thought hadn't even occurred to me

until it came out to pop Chezzie's gloat balloon. Finals? Against BHHS? "Duh? Why not? If I have to go to Salem, why not teach them to act Beverly Hills? Besides"—I held up the Splitflex—"I have this to keep my splits in perfect form. It would be a shame to waste it."

From the looks on their faces, you'd think I'd said I was going to go on *Oprah* and tell all their secrets on national TV. As if anyone really wanted to know.

"Thanks for giving us such a great send-off, girls," my dad said, tapping his watch. "But we have a schedule to keep."

"Right." I climbed into the SUV and strapped in. I waved until I was out of sight, trying not to think about how I would face a new school without Maddie to help me pick out my clothes and pluck the stray eyebrows I sometimes forgot. And . . . never mind. It doesn't matter. I'm going to Salem. And maybe I would meet them at the tournament. But I wish I hadn't said so. Because my comment had changed something. I could see it in the way Chezzie's top front teeth had peeked out of her smile like they did when she thought she had juicy news to tell.

And I could feel it inside me. Would I be a traitor if I cheered against them? It wasn't my fault I had to go to a new school. And I intended to be kewl, no matter what it took—even if it did come down to beating Beverly Hills in the cheerleading finals.

"First stop, Grand Canyon!" Dad announced. Oh, goody. I put in my earphones and turned up the music, the oh-so-appropriate "Boulevard of Broken Dreams," by Green Day. Prepare for a bumpy ride, I thought. Life is so not fair.

Chapter 2

ME: Salem sux News at 11

MADDIE: U dont luv the pool?

ME: Even an indoor pool doesnt make up 4 this crapitude

MADDIE: U need 2 make frenz

ME: Hah! Ppl here dress like Macys on parade

MADDIE: LOL! Cant be that bad

ME: Is Except for punks in black with piercings and hair any color but natures own

MADDIE: Noway Met any witches yet?

ME: Kidding? Not leavin my room

MADDIE: Sounds booooring!

ME: Dont wanna make the rents happy by
tryin 2 fit in
MADDIE: True But if U met a witch U could
steal a broomstick and fly home
ME: Sounds like a plan
MADDIE: Kewl Ill hide U in my closet if Ull eat
my sushi 4 me

Maddie's responses to my useless whining made me smile. Pretty much the only thing that had since I'd left Beverly Hills. Sure, the girl really hated sushi. But she also knew how much I loved it.

Not that I'd seen a sushi place when we drove down the narrow streets of our new home. After the two-week road trip, I'd pretty much taken to tuning out courtesy of my iPod. With my eyes closed, I could pretend I was anywhere but in the back of an SUV, wondering why the very short texts I got from everyone but Maddie claimed they were "too busy." Which meant they had moved on and I should too.

Maddie's texts were all I had left from my life in Beverly Hills. Well, and Mom, Dad, and the Dorklock, of course. But after too much close-quarter *fun* traveling across the country, I was ready to pretend I didn't know any of them.

Mom would have quickly zapped us all to Salem, but Dad had made her compromise. Dad always made her compromise. Which should make living in witch central really interesting.

Rather than traveling in the blink of an eye like the witches we were, we went off for a long car drive across the country. Education, Dad called it. Family time, Mom said.

I would have called it torture, man's inhumanity to witches, and death after life. But if I did, annoying harp music would play. So instead I put on my headphones and turned on my tunes. The pounding lyrics of Disturbed help me tune out the lunacy of my parents. Not to mention the Dorklock.

I'd thought locking him into a moving SUV for long hours would be guaranteed to turn my parents around. But he'd embraced the new "witchcraft is okay" mood in the house. He had tucked away his Game Boy and pulled out his travel chess. Then he'd animated the players so that they moved around the board, mostly brawling and not playing any game I could recognize.

Naturally, that made Dad a little nervous. He kept looking over his shoulder and asking, "Can those people in the van see into our car?" or "Is that trucker watching you or the road?"

But Mom only laughed and said it would be fine, people would just think he had one of those new 3-D games. Right. Okay to animate the chessboard, but we have to drive to our new house. Salem, here we come—the mortal way. Three witches and an uptight mortal.

Under my breath, I had said a little spell. After all, if my brother could bewitch his chess pieces, it seemed only fair I could use magic to make the trip as bearable as it could be.

"Roads be clear of traffic today,
Inns be wired for HBO.
Home is where I wish to stay;
Cure Dorklock without delay."

Although we didn't hit major traffic, and every place we stayed had HBO, the trip was still as painful as I had imagined it would be. Twelve states in two weeks, with a hyperactive little brother and parents who can make the most interesting things sound as boring as oatmeal without brown sugar or raisins.

The Grand Canyon was kind of neat, but the Rock and Roll Hall of Fame and Museum in Cleveland was lame. My brother tried to take a barrel over Niagara Falls, but Mom stopped him with a spell that made him chirp like a bird every time he had an impish impulse. He chirped a lot. Loudly. By the time we got to Salem, we were all a bundle of nerves.

Mom had wanted to zap us to our new house, but Dad insisted on driving. You'd think that would be a no-brainer since we'd already driven cross-country. But the whole witchworld thing really complicated the process. Witches zap, mortals drive. And the witches in Salem don't live in those cute little houses that all the mortals live in. Except for us.

Dad had to go to work every day, and he couldn't zap himself there. So we had to live in a mortal neighborhood and drive a mortal car into a mortal driveway. Which meant we needed some really tricky real estate. Like a house that existed on both planes. There aren't many, and the one we could afford was about four hundred years old and looked like it hadn't been renovated since at least the turn of the century.

"Wowie zowie. This house is cool."

My brother's idea of cool was the twisted, snaking iron fence with gargoyles on the top points. Mine was the pool and the one-lane bowling alley inside. A prerequisite for making the right friends is having a house you can invite them into. This one qualified. Of course, I couldn't do it too soon. Definitely not a good idea to look desperate, no matter how desperate I happened to be.

"How did you guys afford all this? Rob a bank? Or just pop in and borrow some spare cash?" Okay. So I wasn't gracious. But they were lucky I hadn't just walked away on one of the many bathroom stops we took across America. What respectable sixteen-year-old wants to spend two weeks driving from California to Massachusetts "seeing the sights" and being force-fed history?

"We were lucky," my dad answered happily. "The most recent owner was a well-known horror writer who decided to move to Florida permanently."

Dorklock's eyes bugged out. "A horror writer lived here?" The only thing that might have made him happier would have been if Dad had told him there were ghosts his own age in the place. But what Dad didn't know wouldn't hurt him. So no one said a word about the ghosts, who had come to greet us at the front door. Dad's not the most paranormally sensitive guy around, luckily for us.

Unaware that there was a four-hundred-year-old ghost patting him on the back, Dad continued telling us what a great deal he'd gotten on the house. "He was anxious to sell and gave us a great price. Really great guy."

I glanced at my mom, but she was busy greeting one of the ghosts, a younger woman, as if she'd known her forever (while simultaneously trying to convey that they should not bother Dad). Except for her nervousness that Dad would notice the ghosts, Mom showed no signs that she'd been meddling when she shouldn't.

She did that, you know. Even though she told me not to. I could usually make her squirm by asking innocent-sounding questions. Such as, "So, he decided to leave a place like this, which is perfect for writing horror novels, to go to Florida, which is, like, what? The old lady capital of the USA?"

Did Florida even have ghosts? Mom says, next to L.A., it's the least paranormally sensitive spot in the world. Except the North and South Poles. Even horror writers had more sense than to move there.

Dad was not falling for it. He was too happy about finding a house within his budget to question why the horror writer had just up and decided to move. I couldn't tell if he was deliberately ignoring the fact that Mom was talking to thin air, or if he seriously didn't notice. With my dad, sometimes it's best just not to ask.

"Let's say we were lucky," my mom said, breaking off her conversation with the lady ghost, who politely disappeared to let us settle in. I'm not positive, but I thought I detected a faint hint of squirm in her words. "Go pick out a room."

The inside was creaky, but freshly painted. Our furniture was all in place already, thanks to the wonders of witchcraft. It should have made it more comforting to see our belongings in these new walls. But it didn't. Not at all. It was more like visiting the home of thieves who stole our stuff and then used it for themselves. Yuck.

In the car we'd talked about who would get what room. Or, rather, Mom had tried to get us excited about the new place by talking up the rooms. But I hadn't committed. After all, until we actually saw the place, who knew where we'd want to be?

Mom had assured me that there were six bedrooms and I

could pick any one to be mine before I'd taken to nodding without listening whenever she talked to me. (Word of warning: Don't try this at home—one night I ended up with some truly horrific Mexican food because I wasn't paying attention.)

After a tour of the house (I have to admit, it is big . . . if that's a good thing), I picked the room with the turret tower. The curved windows were kewl, as my fellow cheerleaders would say. Or is that used-to-be-fellow-cheerleaders?

It was little consolation that Maddie would be jealous—she'd always wanted a turret room—because I knew she wasn't likely to see it. No one from home was going to be visiting me. Not only because of the distance, but also because trying to keep the witch secret from them would be so much harder here. If I made friends at the new school, at least they would be witches and I wouldn't have to worry about spilling the beans accidentally. *If* I made friends.

Despite Maddie's almost-certain jealousy over my room, I decided to keep it from her for now. The last thing I wanted was her turning traitor and thinking I had a good deal in this move. I'd have to send her a pic soon, though, or she'd never forgive me.

Fortunately, Dorklock didn't want to wrestle me for the room I wanted—he wanted the room that overlooked the porch roof. When I pretended for a minute that I'd changed my mind and I wanted it, too, I thought he was going to turn me into a toad then and there. He really does look like a mini-grandmama sometimes.

Despite the danger, it's too much fun to tease him for me to give it up completely. But I usually don't keep it up for too long. Unless he's really ticked me off. "Relax, Tobias. I want the turret room. You can have the roof . . . ummm, I mean room."

He glared at me again, but then grinned when neither Mom nor Dad said a word. They were too busy hoping we'd accept this change with happy smiles. Right. If my parents weren't clever enough to realize why he'd want a room with easy egress to the outside world, I wasn't going to tell them.

It didn't take long to get my furniture the way I liked it. I tried the bed over in the curve of the turret, and then against the wall opposite. Mom had offered to buy me new stuff, to commemorate the new room (she could have popped me new stuff, but Dad would have had a cow—bad for the economy, he says). I said no, thank you (don't be so surprised—not saying thank you in my house tends to bring down nuclear winter from the 'rents).

Normally, I like buying new things as much as the next girl. But throwing away everything I'd collected in my Beverly Hills life just seemed cold. Not to mention final, somehow. What if things didn't work out in Salem and we went home in a few months? No. I didn't want a new school or a new house, but I couldn't do anything about those. I could, however, refuse new things in *my* room. So my yellow comforter glowed in the sunshine from the curtainless windows. It would have looked pretty if all the light didn't show the stains from when I'd had a sleepover and we'd spilled an entire bottle of red nail polish on it.

Mom would have just zapped the horror-novel-red streaks away. Except that all thirteen girls at my slumber party had seen the stains. Since I didn't want to lie, and Mom didn't want to have to wipe anyone's memories, the stains stayed.

"You could zap them away now. There's no one to see." Mom came in as I prepared to shove my bed back to the turret, where the stains would be mostly hidden.

"You mean I have no friends left, so what difference does it make?"

"Things change, Prudence." Mom's voice had that annoying hushed sound she got when she knew I had a reason to be upset. "Even mortals accept that, and they don't live nearly as long as we do."

"I don't mind change—when it's a good change."

"This is a good change. You'll see." She stood up, her voice getting brisker to signal that she was done humoring me. Of course. She didn't leave behind her life in Beverly

Hills. She was a witch and could pop in to see her friends anytime she wanted.

She pointed to the big heavy pieces of furniture I'd been scooting all over the floor by the sweat of my brow. "For example, one good change is that you can zap them now, you know."

Duh. I'd been using muscle power without a second thought. But I didn't want her to know. "I like feeling the weight as I move stuff," I lied, as I deep-breathed the bed across the broad pine planks once more. "It helps me think." True—of how much I hated this place. But I was wise enough not to say that aloud.

"Suit yourself," she said, turning away. But then she turned back. "Prudence—"

"Yes?" Omigod, here it comes—the whole "give the place a chance, part deux" speech. Part one was bad enough.

"I'd like you to practice your magic before school starts."

I hadn't seen that one coming. Or the scalding rage that welled up at one more überunfair life event. "Great. For sixteen years it's 'Prudence, don't zap that,' and now you *want* me to do magic?"

"I always meant to teach you. It just never seemed the right time. But now it is."

I sighed heavily and zapped the bed into the turret. Maybe my anger made me overshoot, but the bed hit the wall and bounced off. Mom waved her hand and fixed the damage to the wall. Great. I'm not even any good at magic now that I'm finally allowed to do it.

"What's next? Are you going to tell me it's time I learned how to sleep with boys and experiment with drugs?" It was a low blow, but I was so furious. All I could think of was how "witchcraft is not to be used in the mortal realm" lectures were right up there with the abstinence and sobriety lectures parents are so good at lobbing at you the minute you leave the house for a simple trip to the mall or a harmless school dance. At least in my house, they were. Until now.

All the sympathy left her face. Good. "Don't think those protective spells I've put on you will be any different now that we're here—they're not. In fact"—she closed her eyes and lifted her hands in a careless circle—"I've just triple-strengthened them, young lady."

You'd think I'd learn to keep my mouth shut when I'm mad. But, no, I have to make things worse.

Mom wasn't finished. "And now I'm going to find my spell book so I can put a "gratitude" chime on you to remind you that you have it pretty good for a sixteen-year-old." She marched out of the room and slammed the door behind her.

For a minute I stood there boiling, wanting to follow her down the stairs. My mom slammed my door. She hadn't done that in . . . ever. And she said this move would be good for us, that it would make us closer as a family. Right.

I went over and opened the door she had just slammed shut. "I can't tell you how *grateful* I am to be a sixteen-year-old *witch* who was never allowed to use magic and now *has* to!" I yelled after her. And then I slammed the door shut again. Hard. Without magic.

Chapter 3

Going from Cinderella at the ball to Rapunzel in the tower was no fun. But what choice did I have? I couldn't put my plan to be crowned kewl in motion until school started. Needless to say, I didn't practice my witchcraft like my mother told me to—just *because* she told me to and expected me to be happy about it. Of course, like all unfair things, my stubbornness came back to bite me two days into my new life as the Rapunzel of Salem.

For some reason, my new school (Agatha's Day School for Witches, of all the silly names) wasn't impressed with my 4.0 GPA, my cheerleading, or my active after-school schedule. They, it seemed, wanted to test me.

"Why do I need to be tested? Didn't they get my transcripts? How different is this school from Beverly Hills High?"

"All new students have to be tested. It's a very exclusive private school, Prudence. I had to pull strings to get you admitted." Mom seemed to think I should thank her for that. "Besides, last I looked at the course catalog, Beverly Hills High had absolutely no magic on the curriculum."

Mom was very calm, probably being "sympathetic" to my moving pains again. Which only made me want to scream. Her parents really should have named her Painintheass instead of Patience. Which she probably knew, since she'd deliberately waited to tell me about the scheduled testing until it was time to go. No time to find the equivalent of a magic SAT prep course.

"Well, that's great. You and Dad have convinced me I shouldn't use my magic and now I have to learn how to do it in school? There goes my straight-A, honor-roll status."

Mom actually looked conflicted. But then she shrugged. I hate it when she shrugs. It never means anything good.

"We'll see how you do in the testing before we start tuning up the harps, shall we?"

The look on her face dialed my worry meter up to overload. It said, maybe I wasn't going to do so well on this test. Me. The girl who had aced every test since preschool. You'd think it would have occurred to me that a magic school would have magic on the curriculum. Duh.

I repeated faintly, "We'll see how—"

"Prudence." I don't know if she meant it as my name, or as a caution for my behavior, because as she spoke, Mom touched my shoulder and we were no longer in the kitchen. I blinked and swallowed to clear my ears, which felt like I'd just hit high altitude onboard a jet plane. Somehow we'd landed in a small, white-walled room that smelled like frosted-over fireplace ashes. There was a white desk that could have been carved from a glacier. It had a faint mist rising from it. Behind the desk there was a very old, fragile-looking, white-haired woman wearing a white robe with about a million folds in it—a bit like what you'd picture an angel might wear if it came to Earth to visit.

The lady in the white robe didn't look like an angel, though. She was so wrinkled, it was hard to tell, but I don't think she'd ever been beautiful, even back in the Stone Ages, when she was young. And even the most ethically challenged nip-and-tucker in Hollywood would have run screaming from her sagging skin.

"Right on time. Good." The woman unrolled a parchment scroll and dipped a white-feather-tipped pen in a well of white ink with a hand that was as wrinkled as her face. "Name?"

Mom nudged me. "Prudence Stewart." The place didn't look like any testing center I'd ever seen. Where were the desks? The test booklets? The clocks that ticked away the time as slowly as the seconds just before the school bell rang? There was only the old lady, who, for all I knew, was Methuselah's mother—and she didn't look like she'd been happy since Methuselah was born. "Age?"

"Sixteen."

She frowned at me, but her words were meant for Mom. "You waited until she was sixteen, did you? This can't be good. And she's mixed blood. I can't approve what you've done. I don't wonder that it has led to problems."

Great. She was not only unhappy, she was mega-prejudiced. Mom had warned me, but I hadn't believed her. In this day and age I thought that people who still hung on to outdated prejudices would at least keep them to themselves.

But, no, apparently witchworld wasn't as advanced as Beverly Hills, where your blood didn't matter as long as your wallet was well-stocked with credit cards. Although Mom says that's a prejudice of another color—mainly green, I guess.

"My daughter has a lot of raw talent. But she hasn't been schooled—"

"Neglected her, don't try to sugarcoat it. Do you think I was born yesterday?" She cackled at that, which made her sound as if she hadn't been born but had hatched out of molten earth at the beginning of time. "Lucky you didn't have worse happen than the boy playing a few harmless pranks."

"I—"

"Adolescence is a dangerous time for witches. I shouldn't have to tell you that." This time she did look at Mom with a glance that suggested my normally überperfect mother had gum stuck to the bottom of her shoe. "All the trouble you got up to in your youth."

It felt a little weird to see Mom treated like she was about six years old. Not to mention hearing the witch stuff discussed out loud. Most of the time we talked about it in whispers, if we talked about it at all—and never outside the family.

I didn't always think my mom was right, but still, I didn't like anyone else saying so. The old lady thought my mom neglected me because she didn't teach me a few spells? What's the big deal, anyway? So I'm a witch. I have powers. I'm still just a regular person. I'm just not mortal.

Methuselah's mom turned her frown back on me and searched my face like she was looking for zits that were about to pop out—or had heard what I was thinking, which I had a feeling would be a truly terrible thing. She leaned forward. "What's your Talent?" Her words were as sharp as icicles.

You know the expression "tongue-tied"? Well, I was. The old lady's glare said, "Answer wrong and you'll be sorry." And I didn't have a clue what she was even asking, never mind what the right answer was.

"She hasn't manifested one." Mom interrupted nervously, drawing the crank's attention once again.

I wanted to sigh with relief. Until I realized that she knew what the old lady was talking about. And she hadn't mentioned it to me. The anger that started boiling up in me evaporated with one thought: Was there something wrong with me, in witch terms? Was I . . . no. She would have said. I would have known.

Wouldn't I?

"Hasn't . . . ? At sixteen?" The mist rising from the desk got thicker, almost as if the desk were melting under the heat of the old lady's displeasure.

"I can zap things from here to there. Make some things appear. What other powers are there?" Did she want to know if I could disappear? And should I tell her I could— when I was really, really, scared? Like when I was six and a pit bull jumped over a fence and ran after me? Somehow I didn't think that would impress her.

Methuselah's mom frowned—at Mom, not me. "Please, Patience, don't waste my time. Put her in mortal school." She waved her hand, and in the blink of an eye and a pop of my eardrums, we were home. The New England sage and taupe Mom had decorated our new living room in seemed almost dark after the white glare of the testing room.

My knees were shaking a little, but I tried to block out the thought that there was something wrong with me by thinking of the positives of failing my test before I'd even started it. "So I have to go to mortal school?"

Mortal school would mean I could still use my powers covertly to "help" maintain my reputation, just as I had done at home. I'd still have to make friends and find a way to get on the squad. But since I was allowed to use my powers here—

Mom chewed on her bottom lip like it was a sour Starburst. "Of course not! You're going to Agatha's Day School for Witches, East Branch. I just forgot how touchy Agatha can be." She smiled at me with all the confidence in the world—misplaced, in my opinion. "Let's try for lucky number two."

And before I could object, we were back in front of Methuselah's mom, also known as Agatha. No doubt the same Agatha whose name was on the school. Lucky me.

∗

ME: Whatever U do dont let ur dad break the custody agreement if ur mom ever wants 2 move U 2 another school! Testing makes U feel like ur 5 again

MADDIE: But U R so smart!

ME: Not here

MADDIE: Noway!

ME: Way!

MADDIE: XXOOOXOXOXOXOXXOO . . . gtg Coach is givin me the stink eye

I felt a pang of disappointment as I snapped my cell phone shut. I'd hoped for some real lament time with Maddie. But the only thing shorter than her answers were Chezzie's skirts.

The time difference really blew. It was after dinner for me, and I was back in my turret tower doing the Rapunzel pining. Not that Maddie was a prince, but she was my best friend. My best friend whose day ran three hours earlier than mine, putting her smack in the middle of post-school cheerleading practice and unavailable to lament with me. She had promised to set her alarm early enough to wake up and wish me luck on my first day of school, at least. If I had a first day of school.

Even worse than the time-delay friendship was the distraction that had pulled her away from listening to me whine: cheerleading. No such distraction for me.

I had dared to ask Agatha if the school had cheerleading (it does, thank the stars, or I don't know how I'd lock in my kewl). But, as a new student, I'd still have to wait for regular tryouts after the school year had begun. I hadn't had to do that since I made the middle school team in sixth grade. So it made for a little change in my plans to take Agatha's by storm, natch. Luckily, I can think on my feet.

I suppose it was best that Maddie hadn't been able to text too long. I might have slipped and complained about being a stranger in witchland. Then Mom would have had to go wipe Maddie's memory again, which would *not* have made Mom happy. Not that I'm very happy with her, either, after our frostfully delightful session with Methuselah's mom. I would rather have had an anesthesia-free booty lift by the Butcher of Beverly Hills than have had to suffer through the frostbite that came from letting myself be "tested" by Agatha.

Mom had seemed perfectly calm, though, when we popped back in to face the old woman. In the same voice she used to stop Dad from blowing a gasket when witchcraft got out of hand in our house, she said to Agatha, "Test her before you make any decisions, please. After all, we did make the appointment."

Agatha might have said no. I was certainly hoping she would.

But Mom was firm and convincing, unfortunately, when she added, "She has had powers since she was just a baby, Agatha, but I've discouraged her from using them, so no doubt she's a little behind."

"A little?" Agatha apparently had lived long enough that she'd worn out any sense of obligation to be polite. "She has a mortal father. She may not even be a true witch."

"She *is* a true witch, just a bit . . . untrained. I'm sure she'll manifest her Talent soon, with the right education. An education I'm certain that only your day school can provide. I *have* done my research, you know. I found Agatha's East far superior to Delilah's South. I would hate to have to send Prudence there."

Mom sounded unnaturally obsequious. I wouldn't have been surprised to see her bow and scrape, like the people in medieval times had to do. Not that Mom was that old, but Grandmama was, and she sometimes liked to remember the traditions of "the good old days."

"Is that so?" Agatha's narrow eyes got even narrower as she focused them on me. "Catch."

She didn't even twitch a finger and a baseball zoomed toward me, right at my nose. I reached up and caught it. Other girls paid thousands to have a nose like the one I was born with. I wasn't going to risk letting this bitter old hag break it.

"With her hands?" She sounded outraged. And when a bit of spit flew out of her mouth and landed on her desk, a plume of steam flared up with a hiss.

Mom, meek as any good Puritan lass, said, "It wasn't practical to teach her magic in the mortal world."

"Practical. You? A witch who married a mortal and brought up not one but *two* children without a proper education? Sounds like you haven't grown any more sensible than you were at her age." Agatha's scorn was even more impressive than my old principal's when he talked to the kids who graffitied "Beverly Hills Tight Ass" on his office door. I have to admit I was glad I wasn't her target.

Mom opened her mouth to protest, although I didn't know what her defense to what was, after all, the bald and ugly truth, was going to be. Because just then Agatha waved a regal, if skeletally thin, hand. "Leave us."

Mom disappeared before she could even let out a squeak.

"Parents. They always insist their child needs extra help. Do you need help, girl?"

That was easy. "No." It didn't matter if it was true, I knew instinctively it was the only acceptable answer. I counted silently to ten, hoping Mom would pop back in and rescue me from this crazy woman. At twelve, it became clear she wasn't going to.

"Good. Maybe you do have more sense than your mother did in her youth."

I tried to wrap my mind around the fact that this lady had known my mom when she was my age. But before I could, she demanded, "Pull a rabbit from your hat."

"What hat?"

The old bat just made a mark on her scroll and said, "Can you materialize anything?"

I tried to visualize a hat. I tried hard, because one thing I've learned is that if you aren't completely clued in to the subject, sometimes attitude and a confident air can get you extra points. And, clearly, I needed all the extra points I could get. After about ten seconds, a Red Sox baseball cap appeared and hovered in the air in front of me.

"Are you a Sox fan?" She actually sounded friendly for a moment.

"My dad is. He's from Boston originally."

"Mortal fools." Okay. Not so friendly. "Pull a rabbit out of the hat, then, child."

I reached into the hat and tried not to look surprised when I felt something squirming under my fingertips. I pulled out the rabbit. Or what was meant to be a rabbit. It turned out to be a hamster. Not my fault, I swear. I had more experience with my brother's hamsters. The last rabbit I'd seen was the one who went to bed in *Goodnight Moon*.

Agatha didn't seem happy with my explanation, even though I'd smiled my best head-cheerleader smile—the one I'd been practicing all summer and was never going to get to use. Another mark on the scroll, and I was already getting tired of the testing. It's never a good sign when you get tired of testing at the beginning.

She looked at me with cold blue eyes. "Do you need extra help?"

"No. I'm fine." I would have said no if she'd sent two hungry lions at me. She had that effect on everyone, I suspected.

"Good." And we were off again.

All I can say is that the test was exhausting. When things weren't flying at my face, orders were flying out of Agatha's mouth. She wasn't just the oldest, meanest witch I'd ever met, she was also the headmistress of a school that wanted students who could fly, materialize huge objects with the lift of a finger, and play an orchestra of instruments with just a few lifts of the eyebrows and a twitch of nose. I, needless to say, was definitely not one of those students. Although I'm proud to say that my smile did not slip once, not even when the violin bow squeaked across the strings and tangled in my hair.

Somewhere during the hell that was my entrance exam to Agatha's Day School for Witches, she let it slip she had been born during the days of Genghis Khan. And she was the one in charge of running a school for young witches. Not a surprise at all—if you were looking to turn out heartless dictators and megalomaniacs.

Somewhere in between not flying and drawing ungodly sounds from a clarinet and a flute without touching them, I realized witch school was going to be even less fun that I'd thought it would be. Agatha assured me, with a sadistic smile, that the only way to remain on the cheerleading squad—if I made it—would be to maintain passing grades in all my classes.

For the first time since I'd joined my preschool class with

a lunch box and a drive to be the first to be potty trained, I would have tried to fail a test—if I knew what I was being tested on. As it was, I just hoped I'd last long enough to see the end of Agatha and her frozen wasteland of a testing room.

Chapter 4

Too bad Agatha didn't see fit to reject me. Although I know she wanted to, since the letter about whether or not I'd passed the test didn't arrive until the night before school was supposed to begin. The spidery handwriting on the official Agatha's letterhead had had to be translated by a reading spell my mom cast.

I thought Dad was going to have a heart attack when the letter just appeared with a little puff of smoke in the middle of dinner—right next to the dish of green beans. But he settled down quickly—he was trying so hard to take this move and all the changes well. "It looks like we have mail." It's amazing that he can come up with ads that make people want to buy things, because I sure wasn't buying his casual attitude.

But that was nothing compared to what happened next: Mom took a quick sip of her wine and summoned the letter to her with a little smile to Dad that she always used when she wanted to say "I'm sorry" without saying it in front of "the kids." After trying to read it with and without her reading glasses, she sighed and muttered a spell under her breath.

The letter rose from her hands, and a booming voice recited what Agatha had written:

"To the Parents of Applicant Prudence Stewart,
"Greetings and good evening.
"It is with some apprehension that we are admitting Miss Stewart to the junior class of Agatha's Day School for Witches. While her academic skills in math and reading are acceptable . . ."

"Acceptable! She has a 4.0." Dad stood up and shook his finger at the letter, which gently wafted away from the breeze of his fury. I was glad that he defended me, even if he did look silly doing it. The translation spell continued without pause.

". . . we feel that she may have difficulty with her schoolwork in even the most basic subjects of spells, summoning, and potions due to her unorthodox upbringing.

"Despite our apprehensions, we admit Miss Stewart because it is our higher duty to do our utmost to fill in the gaps that sometimes occur when parents cannot, or have not, seen fit to bring up a young witch to use magic in a way that improves the world.

"Please be aware that young Prudence will be required to take remedial magic classes in order to make up what she has missed given her mortal education. We look forward to helping young Prudence become the fine witch we know she can be.

"As outlined in our student-parent-school agreement, to arrive under separate cover, please be advised no tardiness will be tolerated. All illnesses will be investigated by a member of our volunteer medical team before an absence will be excused.

"Yours truly,

"Admission Committee

Agatha's Day School for Witches, East Branch"

It was more a letter of resignation than acceptance. They didn't want me. But school duty meant they owed me a chance to learn what my neglectful mother had failed to teach me. Not that Agatha, from her letter, seemed to think I could learn it.

*

MADDIE: School starts 2moro Sure U dont
wanna grab a broom n fly back?
ME: No brooms only remedial classes 4 me
MADDIE: Noway
ME: Way
MADDIE: Is Salem that advanced? I know we
know more about boob jobs and sides but
ME: Mom n Dad werent happy just movin us
away from everything They had 2 send us 2
this really hard school 2
MADDIE: Sux Want me 2 ask Foxy the
paperboy if he will write papers for U long dis?
ME: Thx but lets just hope my rents realize
the error of their ways n bring us home
soon!
MADDIE: Def Saw ur boy at football 2day Hez
hotta than eva
ME: I heart Brent Send pix
MADDIE: On the way
ME: Sigh
MADDIE: More 2moro gtg

Brent *was* hotter than ever. I stared at the picture of my
not-quite-boyfriend in his football uniform. He'd gotten
taller and had broadened out in the summer he'd been

away with his family. I plugged the phone into my computer and printed out an eight-by-ten glossy and taped it to my headboard. The wonders of modern technology did nothing for this witch. I wanted to pop home. Not that I knew how. Yet.

You'd think it would help to know I could be in close contact with Maddie even though we were on opposite sides of the country. But facing the idea of the first day of school in a new school—in a witch school—I had to admit, it didn't help at all. After all, Maddie knew what she was getting into. Maybe a teacher or two had gone over the wall and escaped, but most of them would be back, teaching the same classes the same way they had forever.

I knew what she was getting into, what I should have been facing. Mom and Dad just really didn't get it, or they'd never have made me move across the country to go to a stupid new school where I was going to be the dumbest student in the bunch. Not to mention the one with the fewest shortcuts to the top skills. I mean, I knew all the workarounds for Beverly Hills. Which teacher to suck up to, which one to use humor on, who absitively posilutely would not accept a late assignment. But Agatha's? Total mystery. Except that I'd be in remedial magic classes. Yuck. Honor society was out, at least until I could get my magic up to speed. And who would elect a class officer from the shallow end of the pool? Thank goodness for cheerleading. *That* was my way to kewl. *That* I was going to ace with a proper cheerleader glow.

I had a momentary twinge of regret that I'd told Maddie. But she wouldn't tell anyone . . . I didn't think. And, besides, she didn't know the remedial classes were magic, so no harm, no foul.

Back in Beverly Hills, it had been almost normal to worry about letting the witch thing slip with my friends. But now it just felt plain weird. Because here I was heading for a school where everyone knew I was a witch and expected me to do magic, and yet I'd never be able to show my face in Beverly Hills again—even if Mom and Dad came to their senses—if Maddie told everyone I was in remedial classes. After all, I wouldn't be able to explain it was remedial magic—Mom would just wipe their memories and leave me back at square one.

It didn't help that Agatha didn't think I could cut it even in remedial magic classes. For that matter, after all that testing—not to mention the inch-thick agreement that landed on the flan just as we were recovering from the shock of the iffy acceptance letter—neither did I. Which is why I spent two hours before school trying to find the perfect outfit. If I'm not going to excel in academics, I'm going to have to find a way to be popular until I make the cheerleading team. Surely, given the fact

I'm from Beverly Hills, fashion is the next best thing.

I didn't think "Agatha white" was the hottest thing for young witches, but I wasn't sure how much black was too much. In fact, I wasn't sure there was such a thing as too much black at all. But I wasn't going to go for the Wicked Witch of the West look—or Glinda the Good Witch, for that matter. One thing I know for sure about fashion: You have to like what you're wearing or you won't pull it off.

In the end, I wore a cute black miniskirt over a pair of fishnet tights paired with my favorite black tee over a turquoise tank top. Casually elegant in an "I'm not desperate to fit in" kind of way. I hoped.

I managed to pump up my confidence enough to make it to the kitchen, where Mom had breakfast waiting. Not that I could eat. My stomach was in knots.

"Are you planning to wear that to school?"

You have to understand my mother doesn't ask with the tone that other mothers ask. There was never any outrage in her voice. She says she's seen everything, but she says it low so my father won't hear her. It bothers him that he's mortal. That he dyes his hair black while she touches gray into hers. I noticed there's a jar of antiwrinkle cream in his medicine cabinet. Which is kind of sad, because Mom could zap him as smooth as any of those nipped, tucked, and liposucked movie stars. If he let her.

But Dad is deep into denying reality. Just like the

Dorklock. Who my mother also asks, with a teensy-tiny lift of her eyebrow, "Are you planning to wear that to school?"

Now, in contrast to my very reasonable goth-lite look, Dorklock is wearing a bright yellow jersey with black shorts.

"Yeah."

He doesn't even have a clue we've crossed a continent to reach a primitive land that has things like snow and ice and cold weather. This nexus between the witch realm and the mortal world is just another place to explore. He even asked, the very first day we moved in, if we would use the fireplace to travel, like they do in *Harry Potter*.

Mom said no, Harry Potter was a fictional wizard, and we'd learn to pop from place to place in school, like other witches. When he started asking what would happen if we tried to pop somewhere there was a wall, I left the room. There are so many things I don't know that I don't even want to think about it.

Knowledge is power, not that the Dorklock knows that, despite all his questions. But you can't be an info garbage dump. You have to focus on the important things. Like how you look. "You don't have to dress like you're in remedial classes, Dorklock."

"Whatever." He grabbed up his skateboard and a bagel and lifted his finger to pop himself into school.

But Mom had other plans. "Wait a moment, young man."

He looked down. "Is my fly open? Nope." He took a bite of bagel and sighed. He was clueless about what her next words would be, although I could have recited them aloud if it wouldn't have gotten me trash duty for the next month straight.

"Let me sniff."

He rolled his eyes and lifted his arm. The stench nearly knocked me over, and I was standing two feet away. I sneaked away from the familiar battle—to Tobias, stick deodorant is something to smear on mirrors, not pits. The Dorklock is not one to look ahead more than a moment or two. Which is why he has broken his arm twice and his leg once in accidents that he could have used magic to save himself from—if he ever had a clue what was going to happen before it did.

Mom said he'd grow up soon enough, that he was just young. But I'd never been like that when I was his age. And don't give me the girl/boy thing either. I didn't act like he does when I was four, and he can't be eight years delayed emotionally, even if he is a Dorklock.

Letting their arguments and counterarguments fade away, I checked the time. It was now or never, because as soon as Mom got Tobias's pits cleaned up, we'd be zapping to school. I took out my cell phone and sent a text message to Maddie. Would she be awake like she'd promised? Or had her alarms failed to wake her so early?

ME: Day 1 C pix How do I look?
MADDIE: U hot chicklie!
ME: Wish me luck
MADDIE: Luck Me 2
ME: Luck
MADDIE: Dont know what III do w/o U

Her reply was only a little delayed. Clearly she had been waiting for my text to come in. I felt guilty when I saw the typos, though. Maddie had practically been born texting perfectly. But not when she was up at 4:30 in the morning. If it wasn't for school, she'd probably never get out of bed until noon. I hate that Beverly Hills is three hours behind us.

Timewise, anyway. In culture, they're light-years ahead. If Maddie approved, I felt sure that I was dressed well enough—even if I was going to have to take remedial classes. Building a reputation on fashion alone is tricky, but it can work for the smart new girl—the one who knows it's the girls she has to impress, not the boys. Choosing the right look is not exactly like signing a non-compete clause, because of course any sensible girl wants to get a hot boy. But you can dress like you'll only go for the available ones—not too short, not too clingy, and no cleavage at all.

"Hurry up, Prudence, you'll be late."

"I can always whip up a turn-back-time charm for us, like

Uncle Buzz showed me." My brother was chirping like crazy.

Mom sighed. "No turning back time until you're in college, young man." She looked at us both as if she were sending us into the jaws of death. "Ready?"

Weird. It was all her idea, so why was she acting like she didn't want to do this now? We stood there for a second, no one doing anything. I had a brief stab of hope that she would come to her senses and use that turn-back-time charm to bring us home. But no such luck.

"Okay. First you, young man. Close your eyes and think of Bart's Middle School." She waved her arm, and he stopped chirping abruptly.

"If I don't like the GNT class, can I transfer to the regular ones?"

"We'll talk about that if it happens." She must have seen the way his nose twitched—a sure sign of trouble to come—because she added, "And if I hear you've caused any trouble, I won't make you chirp next time, I'll make you emit an ear-blasting siren."

"Cool." My brother closed his eyes and popped out of the kitchen. The little twerp wasn't afraid of anything.

"He's really going to give those remedial teachers a chance to earn their paychecks." If witch teachers got paychecks. One more thing I didn't know—and didn't want to know. My head must have been in fashion-no-no worry mode, because I didn't even catch Mom's nervous expression. And I almost didn't catch it when she said, "Actually, Prudence, Tobias was put into a gifted-and-talented class."

Ah. G *and* T—I'd wondered what he was talking about. Now it made sense. My troublemaking brother was in the gifted-and-talented magic classes while I was in the remedial ones. "It's not fair. I was good and obeyed all your stupid rules and I get punished, while he—"

"Are you asking me to hold your brother back because you don't want to stand out?"

"Could you? Just for a little while." Great. As soon as the words were out of my mouth, I wanted to pop myself to the moon. That's just what I need. To look jealous of my little brother. "Never mind."

"Don't worry." Mom smiled at me. "You are going to survive the humiliation."

"That's what you think."

I sighed. At least the Dorklock was only in seventh grade and in a completely different school. I wouldn't have to deal with him for at least seven hours a day. Nine, if I was lucky enough to make the cheerleading squad.

First things first, though—conquering the great unknown and coming home queen of kewl. "It'll be okay, honey, I promise." She hugged me, even though I didn't hug her back. "Just close your eyes and think 'Agatha's.'"

"Should I tap my ruby slippers three times too?"

"Prudence—"

"Never mind." I closed my eyes and thought of Agatha's, trying hard not to shiver at the huge iceberg that came to mind. After all, I didn't want to be the *Titanic*. Not on my very first day.

Chapter 5

MADDIE: Can U stand the new school?

ME: Ill survive Barely

MADDIE: Kewl Me 2

ME: Why? Whatz changed in the same old same old?

MADDIE: Mr Whidbey still hasnt retired Chemistry = a waste

ME: Bummer

MADDIE: Yep Gtg Coach is making us do mega pushups

I stared at my cell phone screen. Great. No one to commiserate with me on my horrible, rotten, no good, very bad day. Alexander had nothing on me. For once I really got what that dumb book was about. Too bad the kids I'd babysat (who'd made me read the stupid book umpteen times a night) weren't around to benefit from my enlightenment.

How bad could the first day of school be, you ask? Well, let's begin at the beginning. The no good, very bad part of the day. With a skill that suggested Agatha had been right to doubt me, I'd popped myself into a closet somehow. A broom closet. What a cliché.

Rather than risk popping into some even more heinous area, I decided to use the common sense I'd learned living in the mortal world and look before leaping . . . or even leaving the closet. I opened the door just a smidge and peeked out.

Lots of lockers. Obviously a gym locker room. The question was, which one? The answer was, I didn't have a clue. The lockers weren't painted pink or blue, just puke greengray.

At least no one was there to witness the humiliating proof that I belonged in remedial magic classes. Thank goodness. Since I wanted to keep it that way, I stepped out and headed for the only door I could see.

Mistake #1. As I reached the halfway mark, success just within my reach, the door opened and a man came through, wrapped in a towel and nothing else. He stopped short, but the soap-scented steam that poured from the room didn't, making my hair frizz on the spot.

I didn't pop myself back home, or at least back into the broom closet. Mistake #2. Why didn't I? Because the man was—how to say it—you know how they do the lighting and makeup so that Orlando looks like he's some kind of young god on screen? Well, this guy looked like that, without lighting. Without makeup. Without clothes.

I was frozen, unable to take my eyes from a bead of water that clung to his left shoulder, just above his collarbone. I was, I admit it, waiting for the downward slide that gravity tends to exert on drops of water on skin.

Apparently, he was not willing to wait that long. "Excuse me, young lady," he said, his voice vibrating on a frequency that got to me. "I do believe you're lost."

"Completely." I agreed. I. Was. Lost. Utterly. Head over heels, lost-my-heart lost. Somewhere inside my head, I knew this was the time I should stammer out an apology and peel off. But I just couldn't. Instead, I zapped the frizz out of my hair and smiled. Mistake #3.

He wasn't steamed—except by the shower. I looked at his face, surprised to see him smiling back. Definitely a star-quality smile.

He held out his hand—the one not clutching the towel to his hip. "I'm Mr. Bindlebrot. Math and physics." He didn't seem to mind that he wasn't exactly dressed for formal introductions. It was hard to say if he even noticed, except that he waved his hand and he was suddenly fully dressed. Which made him look a little more like a teacher. Too bad. He still smelled like fresh soap, though, so I knew I hadn't been hallucinating.

I shook his hand. "I like math." Lame.

"Excellent." When I didn't move, he said, "Shouldn't we be getting to class, now?"

"I'm new." I glanced at the broom closet, hoping I wouldn't have to explain. I didn't want the love of my life to know I was a complete dork. Not until he knew me better. A lot better.

"Aha. Miss Stewart, then, I presume. You have the look of your mother about you."

The look of my mother? What? Did I look like I knew what I was doing? Hardly. I didn't know what to say, so I just stood there. Hoping it was a bad dream—and I'd wake up remembering only the part about him in the towel.

He smiled again, and a dimple as big as a parking lot dent formed in his left cheek. "Well, let's get you where you belong, shall we?"

If only he meant Beverly Hills High. But, no. He pointed his index finger, and I thought he was going to pop me to wherever it is that new students go. Then he said, "Go through those doors"—doors that hadn't been there just a minute ago, I might add—"turn right, and you'll see the main office ahead of you."

"Of course." I went through the double doors, but I couldn't remember whether he'd said to turn left or right, and I was just about to pop myself home—if I could—when I heard voices. Right. Main office.

Apparently, I wasn't the only new student. There were two other kids my age standing there. A guy who was so tall, he had to stoop to get in the door, and a girl who looked exactly like what you'd expect a witch to look like if you were hooked on TV sitcoms from the 1950s. "Ethereal," I think the word is. At least, that's the word my mom uses, followed by the phrase "As if a witch has no use for muscles."

My mom is strong—she goes to the gym every day and works out. She made sure my brother and I did too. She says a witch who depends too much on magic isn't living up to her full potential. Grandmama always rolls her eyes when she says that. Not that Grandmama could be called ethereal. More like man-eater, if you ask my dad.

The two other new students looked at me as I came up to them, with that desperate "Is this a friend or foe?" look that all new students have on the first day, apparently even those in witch school. Gross. I hope I had concealed my desperation better than they had. But maybe I hadn't. Because, come to think of it, Mr. Bindlebrot had immediately known my name.

The secretary behind the desk scowled at me, "You're

late, Miss Stewart." And then she touched her finger to the foreheads of the other students. "Welcome, obey the rules, and off you go." They vanished.

"Now you."

She was surprisingly unfriendly, and I was still dazed from finding the man of my dreams—the nearly naked man of my dreams, at that—so I didn't move.

"Hurry up—do you want detention your first day?"

"Detention?" I hated the word itself. "They have detention in witch school?" Ooops. I hadn't meant to say that out loud.

But apparently I had, because she shook her head. "Of course they do." She reached for me impatiently, and her hand was cold as it touched my forehead. "Welcome, obey the rules"—her finger must have been doing more than poking at my forehead because the school rules flooded into my mind—"and off you go—"

Just like that, I was in the front of a classroom. I was lucky that I'd thought to unfrizz my hair when I was in the locker room with Mr. Bindlebrot, because this was it. The spotlight. The moment when the first lucky group of juniors got to see that I was kewl . . . or not.

The teacher was not Mr. Bindlebrot. In fact, where Mr. Bindlebrot had looked like a young god, this guy looked dead. He was fish white and skeletally thin. A real-life Skeletor, my brother would have said.

"Glad you could join us, Miss Stewart. I'm Mr. Phogg." Even his voice echoed like his lungs were empty of air. Great. And I'd get to listen to him every morning first period. I wanted out of here.

If I'd had any confidence in my popping skills, I would have been out of there for real. Except, as I now knew, unauthorized popping from or to school was against the rules. The last thing I needed was to end up back at the desk with the cranky secretary, who would no doubt send me right to Agatha. I tried not to show the panic that was taking the express elevator from my toes to my scalp. That would be a sure way to get the school buzzing about the new girl—and not in a good way.

Skeletor was getting a little impatient with me. "Please take a seat."

I looked out into the classroom and noticed another no good, rotten thing. Apparently witch kids weren't into goth as much as human kids were. I didn't clash—it would be impossible for my hip but casual look to be at odds with a room full of kids dressed in every style ever popular in the last century or two. Not to mention the ones who looked like they came from outer space. But I didn't fit in either. I could feel it in the way they looked at me with the classic poker faces of kids greeting the new kid in class. And these were the remedial students.

I could have wished myself a new outfit, of course. I

knew how to do that, from all those years of playing dress-up by myself in my room when no one was looking. It was even tempting for a moment, but then it occurred to me that everyone would know I felt out of place. I'd be better off just falling on the floor and drooling if I wanted to make a fool of myself.

And I didn't want to make a fool of myself. Unless it was in front of a naked love of my life, of course. After he'd declared his love for me. And after my mom lifted all her protective spells, more than one of which could cause very embarrassing things to happen if I was to be alone with anyone of the male persuasion for more than a minute.

Of course, she'd never lift the spell if she knew I found a teacher cute. She didn't even like the fact that I'd had a crush on a senior last year, which was nothing compared to a teacher in witch school. But crushes didn't notice little things like the student-teacher divide. Not to mention, since he knew I looked like my mother, the probable five-hundred-year age gap between us.

Skeletor sighed and pointed his finger at the empty desk. Before I could make a move toward it, it swirled up the aisle, circled me, and snapped me up. The ride back down the aisle was excruciatingly slow, as it gave me every opportunity to see the smiles and laughter replacing the dead-eyed looks of boredom.

"Welcome to remedial summoning and spells, Miss Stewart."

He indicated the entire class. "Open your books to the section on summoning."

Everyone busily paged through. I just sat there, trying to decide how far into social suicide I would sink if I raised my hand and asked for a book. Unfortunately, I debated just a touch too long. "Miss Stewart. Please take out your spell book."

There were lots of answers that crossed my mind. But only one popped out of my mouth. "I don't have one."

"What?" The entire room fell silent. You'd think I'd said I didn't have a brain.

"I just started here—"

"I know that," he said, and waved impatiently. "But you should have your family spell book. Didn't your mother give it to you?"

"No." Another omission of my mother's. What was up with this? Did she want me to fail? Did she want me to cement a reputation as a scud in my very first class?

A spell book appeared in front of me and flipped open to a page about a third of the way through. "Use mine for now."

"Thank you." I knew I needed to be polite, but the big, dusty book that now sat in front of me smelled funny. Like it had been buried in a grave until sometime just before class started. The thought of touching it was . . .

"You're welcome. The staff has been warned that

allowances must be made for you." He didn't sound happy about it. But then, I wasn't either—especially now that he'd said it out loud in front of a room full of remedial students. "But I must warn you, Miss Stewart, if your mother has misplaced your family spell book—"

"My mother doesn't misplace anything. I'll have it tomorrow, I promise." I hoped I didn't sound like too much of a suck-up. Just enough that the teacher would no longer think of me as "the girl who was late to her first day of class and didn't bring her spell book either."

"None too soon, I warrant."

The other students giggled, although I don't know why. They were in the remedial class, too, and they didn't have the excuse of a mortal father like I did. I had a not very good feeling that gossip traveled faster in witchworld than it did even in Beverly Hills. Which was bad. Very bad.

It didn't take long to notice my classmates, remedial or not, staring and whispering about me. There was a girl blowing huge bubbles with her bubble gum (in witch school, gum stuck under a desk can be waved away). After the third time she popped her bubble loudly, though, Mr. Phogg lifted a bony finger and waved it away.

"Hey!" she protested.

He merely said, "Today we'll work on summoning a single object." Suddenly, a dozen erasers appeared to hover in a neat row in front of him.

A boy behind me said, "Again? We learned that last year." Troublemaker. I could tell because the deep voice wasn't a whine but a calculated mix of boredom and impatience meant to make Skeletor angry. Which it did.

"We work on it until we get it right, boy." Oooh! Skeletor had this troublemaker's number. "So do us all a favor and get it right today."

The class giggled, and for a moment I felt like I was in Beverly Hills High again, and my life wasn't in ruined tatters all about me.

Anonymous Boy said, "Sure thing." And then the erasers began to fly around the room. I had no time to duck before one hit me square in the face.

"Halt!" The teacher's eerie echoing voice gasped out an order, and the erasers stopped where they were. The one that had hit me had bounced off my forehead and was now suspended in midair in front of my eyes.

"I assume we all know that is not how we get it right." He turned his milky eyes on me. Oh, joy. "Miss Stewart, do you know how to summon an object?"

"I think so." Before witch stuff became a free-for-all in Salem, we had been allowed to do a little in the house—as long as my dad wasn't looking.

"Arrange all the erasers neatly on your desk, if you please."

I didn't dare try to move them all at once, so I carefully

moved them one at a time until they rested in a pyramid on my desk.

"Excellent."

"I moved them all at once," said Anonymous Boy. I just knew he had meant to hit me, but I didn't turn around to give him the satisfaction of knowing I wasn't confident enough to summon more than one object at a time.

"At least she managed to get them all in the correct location. Unless you were intentionally aiming your eraser at her face?"

"I'm not used to anyone sitting there," Anonymous Boy muttered. Creep.

Right. I fought desperately against the urge to turn and give him the stink eye I usually reserved for the Dorklock. If I'd had my old Beverly Hills squad to back me up, we would have made sure he knew he'd dissed the wrong girl. But I didn't. And, as far as I knew, being snubbed by the new girl meant exactly zip. So I decided I'd better be more subtle than that. As we left the classroom, I'd linger for a moment, let him pass me, and then memorize his features for future payback. That's one thing I've learned watching the new kids in my old school: You can't let anyone get anything over on you or you'll be scraping gum from under desks forever. Although I guess in witch school, you'd be popping gum off desks forever.

Chapter 6

MADDIE: Survive D day?

ME: Just

MADDIE: Sux

ME: Big time

MADDIE: Oops Jericho Jake is eyeballing me
No txtin in class C U

I smiled at the phone. Trust Maddie to know how scared I was that she'd even risk having her phone confiscated to check in with me during the middle of her history class. If only I had her here, in my room, so we could put our heads together and figure out my best plan of action to get out of new-girl hell.

Remedial summoning and spells wasn't that bad, although I'd never say that aloud! At home, I'd been the girl who could somehow clean up a mess in a whirl when no one was looking. Here, I was the baby who could barely summon one object at a time, and had no clue how to do anything more ambitious.

The family spell book was like a key to unlock the school, and I wasn't too stupid to know it. I had to wonder how my perfect mother could have forgotten to give it to me. If I couldn't do what the other kids did, I'd never succeed in being one of the kewl kids. I would have been kewl if I'd stayed in Beverly Hills. I was not going to let all that hard work go to waste, even if it meant not sleeping until I had learned every spell in the remedial, regular, and advanced spell books.

Besides, that would give me the means to make sure Anonymous Boy never sent an eraser at me ever again. Assuming I found out who he was. At the end of class, Skeletor waved his thin, bony hand and was gone. Before I could blink, a new teacher had taken his place, new students sat around me, and the room had changed from the remedial spells classroom to introductory calculus. Taught by the locker room god, Mr. Bindlebrot.

I was ecstatic. Not only because I was good at math and even Agatha couldn't deny it, but because my dream man was standing in front of the class writing an equation. It was a simple algebra equation I had learned in eighth grade. No problem for me. I could do it in my sleep.

What threw me was that Mr. Bindlebrot was writing in the air with his finger. And all the other students were also busy writing the same equation in glowing letters on their desktops. With their index fingers. Apparently, only remedial classes needed mortal chalkboards.

I pointed my index finger at my desk and concentrated hard. My equation looked like a kindergartner had written it, and it didn't glow. But you could see it. I solved it as quickly as I could, but the writing slowed me down. I was the last to finish.

Mr. Bindlebrot looked carefully at each person's solution and then zapped it gone with his pinkie if it was right. When he got to me, he didn't comment on the lack of glowiness. Or mention our morning meeting in the locker room. He did, however, zap the non-glowy equation away quickly, before anyone else had noticed that I air-wrote like a five-year-old. My hero.

"Very good! You have a mind for math, Miss Stewart." He said it in a kindly way, as if being able to do the equations was more important than writing them well. I think we both knew that wasn't true, but it was nice of him to pretend.

I'd know how to write my equations neatly in the air by tomorrow's class, with extra glowiness, I vowed. I wanted him to think I was special, not "special," if you know what I mean.

After calculus came lunch. In Beverly Hills, that meant fighting the starving mobs to get a decent place in line so there would be time to talk as well as eat at the varsity cheerleaders' table. At Agatha's, the classroom popped away and we were left in a big hallway with lockers. There was a set of doors that led to the lunchroom. I didn't look for my locker—I didn't have anything to put in it or take out of it. Besides, lunch was one more time when I wasn't stuck with the remedial label on my forehead. I knew how to eat. Time to scope out what was what. And let them scope out what I had to offer: kewl to burn.

I faced the doors, prepared to pick a nonthreatening person to go through line with and charm out a table invite. A little gossip, a little safety in numbers. Perfect for the first day of a kewl coup.

The strategy would have worked in a mortal school. But lunchtime was no different from the rest of the day at Agatha's. Everything was just enough off from a mortal school day that I knew we weren't in Kansas anymore, Toto.

I waited until the hallway emptied enough that I would have some choice as to whom to sit with (the worst thing new kids can do is sit down at an empty table only to find no one else will sit there). I spotted a nice-looking girl to get in line behind—not too pretty, and not ugly. I stepped through the doors prepared to turn around my no good, very bad, horrible day.

As if. Agatha's didn't need a cafeteria that served up over-cooked, underflavored food, or a line to pay for the privilege either. Instead, the room was set with small tables and comfy chairs, and it was filled with the scents of exotic cuisines from all countries and regions. The cultural diversity at Agatha's seemed to include a few cultures that had died out in the mortal world. I spotted at least two guys wearing togas and one in what I swear was bear—not stylish fur, mind you, but the whole bearskin, head and all. More like a declaration of war on fashion than a statement.

The girl I'd followed in sat with friends and evaporated from possibility to impossibility. I did a quick scope of the room to see where I should sit. All my instincts were scrambled, though, because I couldn't tell what group was what in witchworld, except of course for the A-list tables of girls and the A-list tables of boys. They stood out, even dressed in the wide range of styles that passed for fashion sense at Agatha's.

I knew I couldn't try to get in with that group: the kewl girls who sat laughing and chatting over salads. I pegged them for varsity something, probably a mix of mostly cheerleaders, soccer players, and basketball players.

I looked around, trying to figure out the groups. The first thing I noticed was color. It was funny, but one corner of the room had a blue theme going, while the opposite corner was definitely going with browns and greens, then there was the blacks and reds and the silvery blues and grays shimmering in the last corner. The middle of the room contained all the colors, but everyone seemed to have some white element to their outfit, whether it be a white belt, purse, or bleached-white hair. Interesting, but what did it mean? Worse, what did it mean that the varsity tables were a total mix of styles and colors? At least in the street clothes.

Just when I was afraid I was going to have to eat alone—which would have been tricky since I didn't see any extra chairs—I noticed the perfect group. Two girls and a guy.

They weren't scuds (the lowest of the low in any school, even a witch school, I'm sure). But they weren't even remotely kewl. Fringies, no doubt. The kids who deliberately didn't belong to any group, including the one to which they'd naturally belong. My old high school had had its share of fringies. I'd even had one as my lab partner in freshman biology. Doria had been very sweet, very good at taking lab notes, but she hadn't had a clue that she was a fringie by dint of her thick glasses and her habit of walking away without explanation halfway through a conversation. She wasn't a nerd or a geek, she just sorta floated along without any one group.

Speaking of nerds and geeks, the guy at the table I was thinking of crashing was wearing these weird glasses that had three lenses—green, red, and yellow—one on top of each other. I'm not sure what kept him—or the girls he was with—

from falling over the line from fringie into scud territory, but I trusted my instincts. I had to—they were all I had right now.

Anyway, these three seemed harmless and potentially helpful. That was the great thing about fringies. They were just openly curious in an accepting way. They'd talk to anybody without any thought of personal rep. Perfect for a first day lunch that should net me the scoop on my fellow students.

"Mind if I sit here?" I didn't see a chair, but I figured I could deal with that if they agreed.

"You're the new girl." The chubby girl, who was sitting next to the boy with the glasses, smiled as she said it, no nastiness intended. "I'm Maria." She raised her chili dog and took a bite without answering me. Yep. Definitely a fringie.

The other girl, who was skinny and pretty enough to be sitting at the kewl table if she hadn't been wearing a dress that looked like it was made out of a potato sack, just smiled at me faintly, as if she was trying to look past me without being completely rude.

Clearly not an invitation to sit yet. I felt like everyone's hot little eyes were on me, but there is a lot of truth to the saying my mom likes that goes "If you knew how little people thought of you, you'd be shocked." Or something like that.

The boy took a sip of his soda and fiddled with his glasses for a minute before he said, "Is it true you were raised in the mortal realm? That you went to a mortal school?"

"Yes." Was that a good thing or a bad thing? All I knew was that it was true.

Apparently the truth can set us free. Sometimes. A chair appeared in front of me. Duh. Magic lunchroom means magic chairs. I grabbed it and sat for a moment, unsure what to do about the actual eating part of lunch.

I could probably conjure up a peanut butter and jelly sandwich. Or maybe a hot dog like the two girls were having—with mustard and onions. Probably. But I'd rather have what the boy with the weird glasses sitting across from me was having. It looked like a curry. I love curry.

Trying to look like I was just making conversation and not fatally interested, I asked, "Is that from the menu? It looks good. Where's the kitchen here?"

"Curried chicken and peanuts." He didn't sound friendly, but he didn't sound unfriendly, either. I decided to take it as a good sign.

"Looks good."

"Zap yourself up some."

From a few tables away, in a sea of anonymous faces, someone yelled, "She can't. She's waiting for someone to cook it for her, like they do in the mortal realm." I couldn't see who'd said it, but the voice was familiar. Anonymous

Boy from remedial spells. Was this guy going to haunt me for the rest of my life? What a worm. Maybe I'd have to ask Dorklock how to get rid of a pest.

I did what any self-respecting girl does: I pretended he didn't exist.

"You don't know how to use magic?" Curry Boy suddenly looked interested. Figures.

"I'm just rusty—not exactly fair to use magic against mortals, is it?" I had a hunch fairness mattered to this guy. Happily, I was right—or I might just have been skipping lunch from now until the end of the school year. Which would mean figuring out how to get a bathroom pass in this place.

"So you had to do things the mortal way—like cook and stuff? In an oven? Or did you use a microwave?" I recognized the fatal signs of a mortal groupie. I had a few among my mom's side of the family. Annoying souls who thought it was quaint the way mortals (and my family, up until now) did things. I hated being quaint.

"Never mind. I . . ." I wasn't going to get into a session where I had to answer stupid questions like how many mortals does it take to screw in a lightbulb. My grandmother delights in such nonsense, but I *have* to put up with her.

"Let's trade. I'll pop you up some of my trademark curry if you share the secrets of the mortal world with us." The boy stopped fiddling with his glasses. He waved his hand,

and another dish of curry appeared on the table, as well as a can of soda so cold that I could see the sweat running down the side.

Interesting. He could handle two acts of magic at one time with relative ease. I wondered if that was normal for kids our age, or if he was one of the advanced students. One of the advanced students who could be a shortcut to my learning everything I needed to know to take this school by storm.

Taking my hesitation for refusal, he added, "I'll put a quietatus bubble around us, too. That way, they"—he glanced at the crowd at the table where Anonymous Guy was anonymously sitting—"can't hear us."

I sat. Maybe if we exchanged annoying questions, they wouldn't be so annoying. And maybe I'd learn how to whip up some handy quietatus bubbles. Maybe.

The curry was delicious, and Curry Boy (real name Samuel), Maria, and Denise (Potato Sack Girl) made me feel welcome by adding a big brownie with nuts and whipped cream to my lunch.

First things first, I asked the most important question. I cringed a little inside before I dared to speak my questions out loud, thinking that even fringies could recognize a scud. But there really wasn't any choice. I didn't have time to wait to figure out which was the in group to join—or what I needed to do to join it.

"What's with those guys?" I tried not to be too obvious, just cutting a quick glance to one corner. "They look like they were dressed by Mother Nature herself."

Maria laughed. "You're funny, Pru."

"I'm not trying to be funny. I'm trying to learn about what makes a girl get ahead here at Agatha's."

They all three stared at me for a minute while they digested that I was serious.

And then Samuel said, "They've manifested their Talent, and it has to do with the earth."

Oh. The Talent thing again. Great. "Does everybody know their Talent?"

"No. Not everyone." They all looked to one small table, the witch equivalent of scuds. Five people. Even though I couldn't see any difference betweem those five and the rest of the kids, I so did not want to be one of them.

"This whole Talent thing is so weird for me," I said.

Maria nodded. "Yeah. When I found out I could summon fog, I wasn't sure whether to be bummed or happy."

"Why? Fog is handy sometimes, isn't it?"

Maria shrugged. "The Water Talents are not the most respected. But I like that I'm a Water."

"Me too," Samuel said, smiling at her. "Earth and Water make a good team."

"So you're an Earth Talent? What's that?" And why wasn't he sitting over there with the other Earth witches?

Not that I would dare ask that one aloud. I guess it was the fringie thing, lucky for me.

He shrugged. "I'm just grounded."

Denise clicked her tongue against her teeth. "Don't be modest. You already have control over metals and glass." She pointed to his glasses. "I wouldn't be surprised if you one day learned to control magma."

He blushed. Cute. Hard to believe he might one day be able to toss lava at an enemy. More likely that he wouldn't, even if he could. "You're not a slouch yourself. I've never seen anyone grow a black orchid overnight."

It was Denise's turn to blush. "That was just lucky timing. The ground was perfect chemically to support that orchid."

That's another thing about Fringies: They appreciate everyone's unique qualities and say so, whether there's anything to gain or not. I just ducked my head and ate my lunch. Wonderful. I'd picked a table with kids who had all manifested their Talents.

"Don't feel bad. Now that you're at Agatha's, you'll probably manifest any day now." Denise said, as if she knew what I was thinking.

"Wow. It's like you read my mind." I said it partly as a joke, and partly to check if she really could read my mind.

"Reading minds is for Air Talents." She laughed. "All that being an Earth Talent gives me is the ability to read emotions."

Lovely. Apparently, my fear was seeping out. I glanced at Samuel. He smiled. "Don't worry. You *will* manifest soon. Maybe you'll even manifest a Magic Talent. That's the best."

"Why?"

"You can control other people's magic in some way."

"What other kinds of Talents are there?"

Samuel quickly cataloged them. "Magic, Earth, Air, Fire, and Water." He smiled. "Sometimes they run in families, but not always. My dad is an Air Talent, and my mother was a Magic Talent." Definitely a geek.

"Cool." I came back to earth real quick. "How many half mortals manifest a Magic Talent?" And then, a horrible thought occurred to me. "How many don't manifest a Talent at all?"

They all looked embarrassed for a second, and then Maria shrugged. "Not many. Don't worry about it."

Of course I wouldn't worry about it. I'd just obsess. What can I say? It was my nature.

Unfortunately, for every one question Samuel answered of mine, I had to answer two of his. While they weren't completely lame questions, they were mostly classified as "silly myths." Did mortals really have to drink milk or their bones would turn to mush? Did mortals have six toes? Did mortals sleep with their eyes open? Sigh. It was like looking at a fledgling version of my mother's relatives—my grandparents and my aunts and uncles all refused to believe my father wasn't some bizarre creature who belonged in a zoo. Sometimes I felt that way, too, but not because he was mortal.

"Do mortals mind that they die so young?" Samuel asked.

My father's mother was ninety and going strong, but I knew that was nothing compared with my own mother's youthful witch age of 346. "They don't think about it. It's just the way it is." Although, if I were to be honest, I'd have to admit that there was an awful lot of literature around death and dying. They even made impressionable ninth graders read *Romeo and Juliet*.

So I asked a question that my mother and her family avoided when my brother asked (after I put him up to it, of course—he's an easy patsy). "Do witches ever die?" Maybe that would explain why my grandmama calls the bard's teenage lovers "incomprehensible puppies."

Samuel goggled at me. I'd never seen anything but a cartoon goggle before, but there's no other word for the way his eyes popped out of his head.

"Of course we do. But what's the point of talking about it when it won't happen for forever?" Denise shook her head, and I felt like I'd stepped in some deep doggie doo somehow.

"Unless we're killed—usually by mortals," Samuel added darkly. For a minute I thought my curry and my chair were going to disappear.

"She's new, she didn't mean anything." Maria put her hand on his arm.

"No offense." I held up my hands in the universal gesture, wondering if it applied in witchworld. "I just had to test with Agatha herself to get into this school, and I was beginning to think my fate would be to look like her forever—unless she banished me back to the mortal realm for being hopelessly unmagical."

Apparently Samuel recognized my truce-flag gesture. He relaxed and smiled. "You really are new at this, aren't you?"

"I did magic at home, of course," I exaggerated. "My mom homeschooled us in magic, you could say." No way did I want him to know how unprepared I was.

A bell sounded faintly. All the tables and food vanished, and we were suddenly back in the hallway lined with lockers. I thought wistfully of the few bites of curry remaining on my plate.

"They really don't give you much slack here, do they? At least at home they only ring the bell, not make the room disappear."

Samuel, Maria, and Denise looked surprised at the thought of having to move through hallways on your own. "Wow. Don't you get lost that way?"

"Umm, hello? It's a school building. Even if you get lost, you just turn around and try again."

They didn't get it, but they just shrugged and the girls

peeled away to get stuff in their lockers. The clang of lockers opening and closing made for a familiar sound with a real twist. Just like my old school. If we popped from classroom to hallway to lunchroom without any choice, that is.

I took a chance, since Samuel and I had been engaged in mutually assured questioning. Every new kid has to face this moment, usually several times until they know the layout of the most important things—lockers, bathrooms, and classrooms.

"How do I find out which locker is mine?" No way would I ask a boy how to find the bathroom. That question I would save for a girl—and only in an emergency. I glanced around the hallway, wondering vaguely what the other kids were getting out of their lockers. They were witches, they could pop anything they wanted, couldn't they? But I wasn't going to ask. Not on my first day.

"Can't you tell?" He seemed genuinely surprised.

"I'm not psychic."

He flipped his glasses at me for a moment, as if trying to decide if I was serious, or teasing him. I suppose he got a lot of that. But at last he realized I was not about to yell gotcha. "Well, neither am I, and I can home in on my locker."

Great. Another thing I didn't know how to do.

"Home in. Oh. Of course. I didn't realize," I lied. Well, not really lied, but the way I said it sounded like I knew how to home in on something. And that was a pure, charcoal-colored lie.

Which he was very likely to find out, given that he didn't seem to need anything from his locker, because he just stood there staring at me.

"Thanks," I said, hoping he would walk away. No luck. I could see he wanted to say something. For a minute I hoped he wouldn't, but then, when I realized he was going to get the courage up, I changed to wishing he wasn't going to ask me for a date.

Be careful what you wish for. Sometimes what you get is worse. "I'd like to know more about mortals."

Right. Mortal groupie. At least he wasn't gross about it. He even looked like he was a little embarrassed to admit his addiction to knowing all about mortals. I shrugged to show him I didn't hold it against him. "I'd like to know more about magic." Which, I realized as I said it, was very true. I wanted to be able to do what these kids could do when they were in kindergarten.

"We could—" He couldn't seem to get the words out. It was kind of cute, in a fringe geek crush kind of way. Believe me, I've had plenty of experience—guys aren't always so smooth with a girl they like. As cute as it was, I didn't want to encourage him. Really, I didn't. I just wanted to pick his brain while he picked mine. Fair is fair. "Would you like to come to dinner at my house?"

He looked stunned.

Too late I realized my invitation sounded like encouragement, but really it wasn't. Trust me. Dinner at my house would mean I could pick his brain to my heart's content, and all he'd get was a close-up look at a mortal who changed from his three-piece suit to faded blue jeans when he came home for dinner.

"You could meet my father—a real, flesh-and-blood mortal who knows all about witches," I explained, trying to derail any stray hope he might have of doing the boyfriend-girlfriend thing. I knew my mother would approve and my father would freak.

My mom spoiled my dad by marrying him—he doesn't get that geek is a rare taste for most girls. Everyone says my mom was a kewl girl before she got married to a mortal and had my brother and me. Everyone on my mother's side, that is—my father's family does find my mother's family just a touch . . . bohemian, I think my grandmother says.

Samuel had only enough time to unswallow his tongue and say "Where—?" before we popped back into our classes—me, remedial, of course. I didn't have a clue what he was doing—starting fires and practicing putting them out in the Black Forest, for all I knew. All the while simmering the dinner invitation in the back of his mind and probably making it into something bigger than I'd meant it to be. I'd have to slip in a mention of my boyfriend back home—

even if that was a slight case of once upon a fairy tale.

This being popped in and out of classes was getting really annoying—a very bad sign for the first half of the first day of the school year. I couldn't wait to ask Mom if all the restrictions and rules eased up in senior year. Not to mention find out about the family spell book she had forgotten to give me. I wasn't sure I wanted to know what her Talent was. She might say Air, and I'd have to worry that she's been reading my mind for the past sixteen years.

Sigh. Only a half day left before I find out what she should have told me before I left this morning.

Chapter 7

MADDIE: NE hotties 2 ease ur pain?

ME: Teachers count?

MADDIE: Like Duranti?

ME: Better

MADDIE: Whoa! Subject?

ME: Math

MADDIE: Brainiac Only U!

ME: Girls gotta crush Speaking of howz my
boy Brent?

MADDIE: Oops Practice startin C U

I hadn't lied to Maddie. Exactly. The boys at the new
school weren't anything special. But I didn't want to give

her any ideas about me being ready to ditch my boy back home and find someone new here. I was still hoping Dad would come to his senses and take us home, after all.

Which didn't make school any easier to live through. After remedial levitation, my next class was history. Still no Samuel. I didn't know whether it was good that I didn't have classes with him (easier to keep him from getting the wrong idea) or bad (harder to pick his brain).

I did know it was good to have history in the witchworld. My ninth-grade history teacher, Mr. Duranti, who was such a hottie all the girls crushed on him madly, had liked to dress up in cheap costumes to "make history real" for us. The boys had made fun of him, but we girls just drooled. He could have put a clown suit on and we wouldn't have noticed anything but his gorgeous brown eyes.

Mrs. Goode didn't bother to dress up. Nope. She still wore her Puritan gray. Not an inch of skin showing except her round, pink face. Even her hands were covered in thin, gray gloves. Living history in a sense no mortal could ever understand.

We were starting with the Salem witch trials, apparently, as there was a large burning stake in the middle of the classroom.

"If I ever hear of you talking about how witches were burned at the stake in Puritan England or America, I will sentence you to a day in the stocks." There was laughter from the other students, but since actual stocks were in the corner of the room—a Puritan punishment device that looked hundreds of years old and probably delivered terminal splinters—I decided to see whether they were laughing because they knew she was joking or because they were sickos who looked forward to seeing fellow classmates tortured.

"The preferred method for killing witches at that place and time was being hanged by the neck until dead. Only the medieval Europeans made a sport of burning witches. Barbaric, these mortals, but they did find our weak spots. We do need to breathe."

A girl sitting behind me laughed. "What about splashing water on us?"

"I'm melting! . . ." The Wicked Witch of the West appeared in the air above us for a moment, and we all laughed.

"*The Wizard of Oz* is a mortal work of fiction." Mrs. Goode sighed, but didn't look as though she was about to sentence the offender to the stocks. "I cannot believe that you are susceptible to that drivel, Miss Martin. But let me assure you that the world will benefit from you taking a shower once in a while."

The class laughed more loudly. I looked at Mrs. Goode closely. Her authentic Puritan dressed-to-overkill style couldn't quite disguise her jolly nature, which was reflected in her round cheeks and twinkling blue eyes. The stray white curls escaping her tightly tied bonnet made me suspect that she'd lived in Salem during the witch trials, and not as a child, as my mother had, but as an adult who'd lived through the mortal madness. Even though Mom didn't like to talk about it, I'd picked up quite a bit just listening to the grown-ups when they thought I was busy watching TV.

It was mainly mortals who suffered the persecution, I hasten to add. But a few witches were swept up in the nonsense. Those who had infections that prevented the use of their powers. Or maybe those, like me, who didn't have a clue how to use their powers to full effect.

It always got me that the mortals couldn't look past their hatred to see that if the witches they tried had the power they claimed, they would have escaped. But I'm not claiming that only mortals suffer from a lack of reason. My mother's family proves that to me on a weekly basis. Which was why it was no surprise when I popped home, tired enough to sleep on a bed of nails, to discover that my grandmother had come to visit.

Grandmama was in the kitchen with Mom when I appeared, fresh from the locker corridor, where yet again I had not been able to locate my locker.

Mom looked worried. "How was your day, honey?"

"Oh, don't ask silly questions, Patience. She was at

Agatha's and mercifully unprepared after that pitiful mortal education you subjected her to."

Mom opened her mouth to object. Probably she was going to say I was a strong young woman. So I struck first. "I didn't have the spell book. They almost sent me home."

"You forgot to give her the spell book?" Grandmama scolded. She looked delighted at my mother's error.

Mom looked horrified, which was somewhat gratifying. "I completely forgot. You'll have it tomorrow, I promise."

"First day of school and you're already making certain she looks a fool." Grandmama says things that, coming from other people, would be offensive. Somehow, from her, they just seem like those fake slaps in the movies: lots of sound, but no actual contact. I don't know how she does it. But she does. Usually. There are times when she connects with a verbal slap that makes your ears ring. But usually that's just with Mom.

She held out her arms to me. "Come here, sweetling, I have a surprise for you." I was glad to see her. Beside the fact that she usually made life interesting, she had deflected Mom's questions. Always a good thing.

"What about me?" The Dorklock had appeared and, as usual, immediately had begun demanding his share of whatever our grandmother had brought.

"Not yet. When you're older. This is just for your sister."

I couldn't help being pleased. Just for me? I couldn't

remember a time when . . . and then, with dread, I did.

When I got my period. I had to go to this horrible witch's camping trip to the top of Mount Vesuvius. Yuck. Bad enough to suffer PMS for the first time.

"What is it?" I smiled as I asked, because Grandmama had been known to turn people into toads, rabbits, or frogs when she was displeased. Even older witches watch out for her temper. Especially when she's just enjoyed hundred-year-old brandy, her poison of choice at family celebrations.

Mostly she did the transfiguration bit on my father, but there was a time when she turned me into a rabbit for spitting up on her. I was only a year old, and my mother made her promise never to do that again . . . but promises and Grandmama never seemed to last. She always assured me that I was a cute little bunny, white with an adorable pink nose.

Disturbingly, that does make me feel better.

She'd promised never to turn Dad into a frog again—but the next time she was mad at him, she turned him into a mule. Technically, I guess, that wasn't breaking her promise. Which is why we've all learned to be careful around Grandmama.

"Come here first, and give us a hug."

I love to hug my grandmother, even though she is all sharp angles and bright colors. When I was a child I thought she was some huge toy that my mother occasionally conjured up to amuse me. "Hello, Grandmama."

"Pet." She hugged briskly, leaving a lingering scent of jasmine in my nostrils. She shook the folds of her latest fashion creation, a bluish-green sea-foamy thing and I suddenly understood why she always says she likes to flow like water. I would have asked her if she had manifested a Water Talent, but just then she waved her hands in a wide, magnanimous circle. A set of keys appeared in the air between us, and suddenly I couldn't breathe.

"Grandmama!" I reached for them, my heart in my throat. A car would almost make up for being uprooted from all I knew and loved. A car would mean—

"Mother, what are you thinking?" Mom casually summoned the keys to her hand and glared at my grandmother.

This was normal behavior for them, but today the stakes were huge for me. I wanted whatever went with those keys. Although I did wonder what kind of vehicle Grandmama would think was right for a sixteen-year-old.

"I'm thinking that the child needs something to make her stand out to her classmates in a way that being in remedial magic will not."

My mother began, "Perhaps in L.A.—"

Grandmama waved her silent. "Oh, pooh. In L.A., everyone had a car. Here, it's exotic."

"I'd expect you to think it was tainted with the whiff of

mortality." Which really wasn't fair. Grandmama adored mortal gadgets and had collected at least a dozen traffic tickets driving very fast around L.A. when she decided to visit in "mortal drag."

"Well, that's why I chose a Mercedes SL600 Roadster."

"A Mercedes!" I looked at my mom, willing her to see what this meant to me—even though I wasn't completely certain myself. My grandmother had excellent instincts when it came to knowing what would make one popular (although, surprisingly, she didn't always choose to be the most popular one in the room).

Wise to my mother, as always, Grandmama asked me sharply, "So? We know you were left appallingly unprepared without the spell book. How complete was your humiliation today?"

"Complete." I knew what Grandmama was up to and I was willing to play along. "I popped into the boys' locker room instead of the main office, I couldn't do a basic summoning spell, and at lunch I didn't know how to conjure up an appetizing meal. Everyone thinks I'm a complete dork."

My mother sighed. "You two always gang up on me. But very well. You can have the car."

I didn't rejoice right away, because I could see in her eyes what was coming next. "As long as your father agrees."

Dad said no at first. Duh.

Grandmama had decided the S Class I needed was bright

yellow, with caramel-colored leather upholstery and a really crank sound system. In L.A. I'd have been kewl plus, for sure.

In L.A. Here, I wasn't sure that I'd be much more than barely cool.

You see, in my experience, there are clear levels in high school. The top of the heap are the "it" kids. They're like the movie stars of high school. Everyone knows who they are without asking, wants to talk to them, and secretly wants to *be* them. Usually these positions are reserved for sports stars and cheerleaders.

The next level is the übercool kids. These kids dress fine, are active in something, and have personalities that work like magnet spells. You can't help but like them, even when they're making fun of you.

Next come the cool kids. They dress well, but aren't active. You like them and want to dress like them or have your hair cut like them.

Next are the geekoids. No one wants to look like them. But we recognize that they are the ones who speak the language of the tech gods. Without them, computer viruses eat our term papers, and cell phones get stuck calling the North Pole.

Then there are the rebels. From the fifties icon James Dean on, they're always the same. They dress like they want to stab you in the heart and take being a loner to absurd heights. The rebels are not fringies, just to be clear. The fringies could belong to any of the groups, but they just don't try. They're missing the "flock together" gene, I guess.

Last, and least, the scuds. They might be on a sports team as towel or water bearer, or sometimes even bench warmer. They might occasionally get straight A's. But they're individually invisible. Groups of them scud through the halls, into classrooms, and onto buses.

I didn't want to be a scud—or whatever they called the equivalent in witch school (which I didn't even know yet— not a good thing). I mean, it was really cool that Wonder Woman could make herself invisible. But she controlled it. Scuds not only have no life and no shape, they also have no control.

Right now, I'm on the cusp. I could become a scud. The thought is scary. The temporary notoriety that protects me from being relegated to the scud faction—caused by living like a mortal for sixteen years—could fade. Will fade. And when it goes, I need to make sure I end up standing out. Even the Mercedes isn't enough.

I figure I have a month before the infamy fades. A month to figure out the spell books, the witch kid hierarchy, and how I can get to the top. If I can't, then I hope I've convinced Dad about the car, because I'm going to need it to drive back to L.A.

First, though, I have to figure out how to make my own lunch appear in the cafeteria tomorrow. I didn't want Anonymous Boy making fun of me again just because I couldn't feed myself.

"Any homework?" Mom asked, trying to pretend a car was no big deal. Sometimes she acts übernormal when my eccentric grandmother is around. I can't be blamed that I decided to tweak her.

"I have to learn how to conjure different dishes. So I thought I might make dinner tonight." Nothing like adding a few brownie points to the record.

Mom looked at the carrot that she was scraping. "I was going to make beef stew. . . ."

"I need to use magic."

She bit her lip. I think Mom was having more trouble with the new rules than I was. Good. She deserved it for moving us all here.

"It's homework, Mom." Which wasn't strictly true—but if I wanted to be an it kid, I darn well better be able to whip up more than pb&j at lunchtime. So I felt justified.

She smiled. "I guess I'd better get used to this new reality, hadn't I?" She dashed her hand, and everything she'd had on the counter to make the stew quickly went back into storage.

"How do you manage to control so many objects at

once? I can barely summon one thing at a time. I was the worst kid in my remedial class today."

"A little practice will put you ahead of all of them, Prudence. Don't be discouraged."

Seeing an opportunity to lay guilt, I sighed. "Oh, right. You mean I wouldn't be in remedial spells if I had been allowed to learn and practice my powers when I was young."

"You're still young." Mom often refused to admit she wasn't perfect. "And I think it is wonderful that you intend to practice what you learned at school tonight for your family."

Oops. Problem was, I hadn't learned it. I just knew I needed to. Second problem was how to get Mom to show me what I needed to know without letting her know that.

I pointed to the dish cabinet and painstakingly set the table one dish at a time. When Mom didn't help right away, I let a dish wobble.

"Here, honey, let me give you a tip." She held up her hand. "You know how you learn to count on your fingers when you're little? The principle is the same." She extended her index finger and a dish rose from the table, then her middle finger and another rose, then her ring finger and a third plate began to hover above the table. She used her pinkie to raise the fourth and last plate and then quickly sent them back to the cupboard.

"Now you try." The door to the cupboard containing paper plates opened. "But not with my good dishes."

I felt like a baby, but the finger method worked surprisingly well. I moved four paper plates at one time, four plastic cups, and four napkins.

By the time I got to the silverware, I was ready to use both hands and moved forks with one hand and knives with the other. I felt like I'd run a marathon. Not that I've ever run a marathon, but I've seen the runners at the end panting and exhausted. I felt like they looked. And all I'd done was set the table.

At least Mom hadn't caught on. She thought she'd offered me a tip, not given me a crash course. Let's hope she continued to think that.

I pointed to the table and thought about beef stew. A pile of peanut butter and jelly sandwiches appeared on one plate.

"I think your father and brother would like—"

I didn't even let her finish. I lost it, right then and there. Which meant, of course, that I burst into tears. "I was thinking beef stew."

Mom clucked her tongue in that annoying way she has when she thinks she understands what's bothering me. As if she could. She's never been half witch/half mortal, and when she was my age she could summon a dozen objects without breaking a sweat. And that was while wearing that itchy, heavy, Puritan wool too. (She's shown me her old school clothing—it was when we were arguing over whether I was allowed to wear belly shirts to school or not . . . ended up not, of course.)

"I'm going to fail!" I wailed, knowing that Mom would think I meant my "homework." What I really meant was finding a place in my new school.

"Nonsense." Mom waved away the pitiful pile of sandwiches—which were grape jelly, not even strawberry, my favorite. "A stew is ambitious, honey. Start with something simple. How about a nice roast beef? That's easy, and your father loves it."

I stopped sniffling and closed my eyes, picturing roast beef like my mom serves my dad on his birthday. Crackly, sizzling, I could smell it. I opened my eyes. I *was* smelling it, because there it sat. Right in the center of the table on my mom's favorite serving platter. "Did I do that?"

"You did." She smiled so indulgently, I was suspicious.

"Did you help? At all?"

"Not even a smidge, honey. It's easier in the beginning if you use something you know really well, which is why I suggested roast beef. Now try something to go with the roast beef."

I closed my eyes again and thought of roasted potatoes

like my mom usually makes to go with the roast beef. Garlicky, crispy outside and sweet and tender inside. I peeked, and was gratified to see a bowl of potatoes on the table. Maybe this wasn't as hard as I'd thought.

"Don't forget a vegetable. Every balanced meal should have a vegetable."

I'm not that fond of vegetables. But broccoli was least objectionable. My brother used to call them trees when he was younger, and I'd softened toward it. Somewhat.

I closed my eyes and thought of broccoli: green, tree shaped, cooked to the point that it was not too chewy or too soft. My mom gasped and there was a cracking sound. My eyes flew open. There was a gigantic head of broccoli planted in the center of the table, which had buckled under its weight.

"Mom!"

She raised her hand as if she was going to wave it away, then stopped and shook her head. "Close your eyes and think of it smaller. *Much* smaller."

I closed my eyes and thought of it gone. Then I thought of peas. Tiny, perfect, round green peas. When I opened my eyes, there was a bowl of peas on the table—sliding toward the huge crack in the center of the table, along with the roast beef and potatoes.

Without consciously thinking of what I was doing, I chanted:

"Table, table, cracked tonight,
Mend and restore to whole again.
I need to make things right,
And practice perfection."

It was probably the ugliest spell I'd ever heard, and certainly not worth recording in the family spell book for posterity. However, the table fixed itself with a soft creaky sound. Just in time, too, because Dad and Tobias came in.

"What's going on here?" Dad smiled his "I'm not suspicious, not me, unh-unh" smile and waited in the doorway for an answer. I think he's just been surprised by magic once too often in his life with my mom.

"Dinner is ready," Mom said. Which was the bare truth. But not really what was going on. And she gets mad when I get creative with the facts—who does she think I learned it from?

"Why are we using paper plates?" Dad asked.

"I was practicing my homework," I said. "But look what I learned today." I raised the paper plates from the table with one hand and opened the cabinet and summoned four of Mom's good plates to the table.

It took all my concentration, but it was worth it to see my brother's look of awe.

"Wow. All they taught me to do today was how to do my multiplication tables in the air."

"Multiply this, then," I said as I sailed the paper plates toward his head.

"The food is getting cold," Mom said as she stopped the plates an inch from my brother's outstretched hands and sent them back into the cabinet. "And we want to do justice to your sister's first meal."

"You made this?" Dad looked at the food—which looked good, I can say with pride. He picked up one of the plates and looked around the kitchen, which was spotless. "You zapped this?"

"Yep." I said it with a big grin on my face. Dad would go out of his way to be nice if he thought we were proud of something—even the most bizarre pencil holder made of dried macaroni and pencil erasers.

As he started to carve the roast gingerly, revealing the perfectly pink center, I said, "I think I'll get an A on my homework tomorrow. Don't you?"

His voice quavered a little as he said, "Of course you will, honey."

It made the roast beef taste even better to see how he sampled everything carefully, as if he was afraid that, no matter how it looked, it would taste like dog doodle. Revenge could be sweet, I found, as I crunched a potato in my mouth. Serves him right for letting my mother drag us here in the first place.

I had a feeling that it was going to be a pleasure to work

hard on my homework in the future. And just maybe the better I got at magic, the better the chance that my dad would end this futile experiment to civilize the Dorklock. Which may have been why I announced, "In fact, I'd like to ask a new friend to come over and help with my home-work."

"A friend? Already? I knew you could do it, honey," Dad said with a big smile. "What's her name?"

"It's a him, actually." I'd known it would be problematic to bring Samuel home to meet the 'rents. Mom would treat him like she did all my friends: as a possible interrogation target to find out more about me. No way would she approve of me using him for his brains and then moving up in kewl status without him. Mom just didn't get these things, no matter how often I explained them to her. And no wonder: It had been centuries since she was in school.

But, Dad, just like I knew he would, freaked, thinking I had a boyfriend at last. "A boy? Great! What's his name?"

Sure, Dad, that doesn't sound like false enthusiasm. "Samuel. He's really good at magic and he's going to help me rev up the studies."

I don't think either of them believed that Samuel was strictly a study buddy. I don't know why. They should know by now that I'm like my dad in one very important way: I'm a type A on overdrive. And if I couldn't find a way out of remedial classes, I was not going to be happy.

Samuel was my shortcut to regular magic classes. So no matter how freaked my dad was, that boy was going to come to the house as often as he could and teach me all the things I should have learned growing up but didn't because my mom wanted to pretend she was mortal and my dad couldn't handle magic.

There are ways around my dad, and there are ways to make my dad as stubborn as the mule Grandmama once turned him into. Pouting worked only when I was very little and cute. I was going to have to try logic.

I waited until dinner was cleared away and dessert had sweetened everyone's mood. Then, I went for the earnest, hardworking approach. "What do I have to do to prove that I'm ready for a car? I get good grades." At least, I did when I didn't have magic on the curriculum, but I wasn't going to go there. "I never break curfew or go over my anytime minutes. I haven't even sent Dorklock—"

"Don't call him that."

Oops. I smiled at my brother, who scowled back at me. "I'm sorry, Tobias, I shouldn't call you that now that you're in the gifted-and-talented program." I forgot that my nickname for my brother made Dad mad on two levels—the one where he remembered his children were witches, and the one where family unity and harmony had a glitch. Try again. "What else can I do?"

"Well . . ."

I could see his mind turning over all the things he might require of me, and I started to envision all the chores he could give me. Raking, mowing, snow shoveling—yuck. And I'd have to do it all the human way. Because I should value the fruits of my labors. Or something.

"Let me think about it."

That would be dangerous. But I didn't see any other option. "Dad—"

"Monday. I'll tell you on Monday."

It was all I was going to get. "Thanks, Dad." He liked that.

"And no nagging. One mention of this before Monday—"

"I know. Results in a cold war."

"And no car." Sometimes he feels the need to let me know just how little he thinks I pay attention. Now I just had to keep Grandmama away from him until Monday. If I could convince her not to turn him into anything, I knew I could get him to say yes to the car.

Chapter 8

MADDIE: New look?

ME: Salem subtle

MADDIE: Aha! U found a hottie

ME: No Just my locker

MADDIE: LOL! Miss ya

ME: U 2 Tryouts soon Send luck

MADDIE: No luck Come home

ME: I wish

I wasn't sure Maddie had approved my new, more Agatha-appropriate look. And, really, even if she had, I wouldn't know if the subtle combination of earth and water tones, with just a hint of cherry red in belt and shoes, would signal that I belonged somewhere at Agatha's. But at least she'd noticed my attempt to dress to build rep. The only way to find out, however, was to try it out at school.

Apparently, after the first day of school, we just pop right into the hallway with our lockers (which might explain my mis-pop on the first day, I guess). Despite the disorientation of one minute being in my kitchen and the next in a bustling hallway filled with the sound of slamming lockers, it almost seemed like home. Almost.

I am ashamed to admit that I actually asked the Dorklock to show me how to home in on the locker. He did. Or so I hoped as I closed my eyes, stood on my toes, and whispered, "Me, Pru the wow wow wow, to locker now now now."

I felt a split second of stomach up the nose, and then nothing. I opened my right eye just a tiny crack. Wonder of wonders, he'd actually told me the truth. Maybe I should start calling him Tobias?

Nah.

I opened my eyes all the way. Locker 666. Great. Even better, it took me three tries to get it open and stuff in it my nearly empty backpack, all the while worrying that I'd get sucked out of the hallway and into class before I got the door closed again.

I kept out only the huge family spell book for my first class. The spell book weighed twice as much as the backpack, anyway. Other than tampons, tissues, a little lipstick, and mascara—the typical emergency supplies for a female of sixteen—there was nothing else in the backpack.

We didn't need paper, because we wrote in the air, except for homework essays and tests—for which, oddly enough, we used the prosaic mortal technology of laptop and DSL. Go figure.

We didn't need pencils because we used our fingers. We didn't need books, except the spell book, because we were hands-on learning all the way. Studying the Salem witch trials? How better than to have your teacher zap you into the past to observe the proceedings? Two-minute oral presentation at the end of class. Twelve-page paper due next week.

You might wonder why witches need lockers. Why not just zap our spell books to and from home as we need them (no more forgotten homework, a big plus for all involved)? But the mortal world's television has colored even the witch idea of what is appropriate.

And a school lockdown to "protect the innocent children" has nothing on Agatha's. Forget metal detectors and hall passes made by the shop teacher. Every student is bound to the school with a series of spells that would make your eyes cross if you had to recite them.

Last night, I had decided to read the student-school agreement I'd signed under duress (a stack of small print that gave away all my freedom and stuck me with a ton of responsibilities that I didn't want). I'd thought the rules that had popped into my head when the school secretary stuck her finger on my forehead were bad. But the fine print was even worse. Nevertheless, I read on. Know your enemy, Dad always says. In school—as in the advertising business—the enemy can be anyone.

No unauthorized popping of any kind. No flying faster than a walk. No interference with any and all of the magic spells that keep us in line. In other words, we had all these great skills we had to master, but we better not have any fun doing it, or else. It must be really frustrating to the kids who aren't still learning remedial skills.

Of course, like schools anywhere, at Agatha's they made concessions to make it seem less like prison. You know, like making nasty medicine purple and pretending it's really grape flavored? Ergo, lockers, desks, and pep rallies. Oh, joy.

The high school not only had a football, basketball, hockey, and soccer team, it was in a vast cooperative with mortal schools. Although the biggest competition was with the other witch high schools, there weren't all that many of them in the country, so the Salem team practiced against the mortals, with magic strictly prohibited, in preparation for the witch-witch matches, where magic was not only allowed, it was necessary (when the Area 51 Flyers got mad at a ref call in a contentious soccer game and conjured a fire-breathing dragon, the plaque in the trophy hallway proclaims, the

Salem Witches matched and beat it with a fire-eating hippo with fireproof hide and a nasty temper).

The pep rally for the upcoming game (against the Washington Black Arts) answered all my questions about what to do to get to "it" status. But not so much about how to do it.

"If you think you have what it takes!" Coach Gertie, the cheerleading coach, shouted as she waved pom-poms.

"If you think you can add to the team!" the football coach shouted and rallied his returning players.

Together, the coaches shouted, "Then try out!"

I watched the cheerleading team closely. They were cute girls, but they were mondo uncoordinated. They did a basket toss that looked more like a basket-with-a-hole-in-it toss (the flyer didn't hit the ground—but only because she used magic when the four girls who were supposed to catch her misjudged her landing by at least three feet).

"I'm going to try out for soccer," Maria leaned over and whispered to me. I'd managed to snag a seat next to her somehow—the one person I knew in the crowd. Although Agatha's wasn't as big as you might think. Witches aren't rabbits when it comes to kids, I guess.

I smiled, suspecting strongly that soccer in the witch-world was as basic as it was in the mortal world. Kicking a ball. How hard is that? But then the soccer team came out on the field and I changed my mind. Apparently in witch soccer, you weren't allowed to use your hands or feet—only magic and, occasionally, your head. "Good for you. I'm going out for the cheerleading squad."

She looked at the girls on the field, who were at the moment misspelling victory—the Y was missing. It seemed like an omen. Like fate saying I was meant to be the Y in victory at Agatha's. Maria's eyes widened. "You're brave."

"I was on the team at my old high school." I didn't mention that I would have been captain this year if it weren't for my Dorklock brother and overprotective parents. Maria might spread the news around. And while that could give me kewl points with the rest of the school, it would make the cheerleaders hate me. Big-time. That news had to wait until I was one of them.

"But that was a . . . ," she whispered, "mortal school."

"So? Cheerleading's cheerleading, isn't it? Hurrah for the team! Win! Win! Win!"

"I guess so." She shrugged. "Good luck."

For a minute I wanted to point out that one couldn't be an it kid if one didn't go for it. But I suppose that's something Maria the fringie soccer player, wannabe or not, could never understand. I mean, I get that some kids don't really want to be kewl. Obviously. But I'll never get why. That's beyond me.

Tryouts started on Friday. Signups were in the main hallway, natch, since other than the disappearing and reappearing lunchroom, that was the only place we'd all be at the same time. The only hitch was that Friday was three days before I'd know whether the Mercedes would up my kewl factor or not. It was a calculated risk. And, if I thought it would sway the decision, I could always anticipate my father's agreement and lie about the Mercedes.

I zapped my signature onto the tryout sheet, and a big index card with moving pictures on it appeared in my hand.

The card said WHAT YOU NEED TO KNOW BEFORE TRYING OUT FOR THE TEAM. I stuffed it into my pocket because the lunchroom doors had finally appeared and everyone was filing in from the hallway. I'd been a cheerleader since the sixth grade and I'd only been magicking food for about a nanosecond.

Feeling confident that my work with last night's dinner had made me lunchworthy, I looked carefully over the crowd in the lunchroom today.

I'd seen the current cheerleaders at the pep rally. Many of them sat at a table together. They just looked like cheerleaders, laughing and commanding the attention of whoever looked in their direction. Soon, I thought. But not today. Not until after I made the team.

But where then? Not at the tables where Anonymous Boy lurked. It was a real pain, I realized, that I hadn't manifested my Talent yet. I'd have a place then. Of course, I might not like it, if, for example, I had to wear those earth tones everywhere I went just because I happened to manifest an Earth Talent.

I stood dithering for too long. At last, judiciously, I decided to sit near Samuel, Maria, and Denise again. I had yet to finish the invite I'd started to give Samuel to dinner.

Speaking of which—I'd reconsidered the dinner thing. I needed more than a little munch time with him if I wanted to get out of remedial classes. I needed us to be study buddies. Lunch would give me the time I needed to make him think he was asking me for a favor (a trick I learned from watching Grandmama).

I sat down with them as if it were expected, popping a chair for myself without breaking a sweat. I doubted anyone watching would guess I'd practiced the move for an hour and a half the night before. "Hi." I dialed the smile up to bright for Samuel. "I wanted to thank you for the curry yesterday. It was delicious."

"No problem. It's my mom's favorite recipe. She made it a lot before she died."

Died? Was his mom a mortal? Not likely. But when Maria and Denise both looked at me with crazy big eyes to warn me off, I remembered how he'd said witches sometimes get killed by mortals. Not a subject to surf at lunch.

Which didn't mean I wasn't insanely curious, but if I asked, I could forget him as a study buddy, never mind get him to come around to thinking the favor I needed from him was a favor he needed from me. Dilemma.

Stalling, I said, "Can I offer you a slice of my mom's

chocolate cake? It's to die for." Great. *To die for.* What was I thinking?

He stared at me for a moment. Fortunately for me, he wasn't the type to take offense when a cute girl (I'm not being vain, just accurate) said something truly dumb (see, I don't have a problem with my good points or my bad). "Sure. I love chocolate cake."

Excellent! I had practiced this last night until even the Dorklock had asked me to stop. I popped a perfect piece of chocolate cake in front of him—and one in front of Denise and Maria, since they had added the brownie and whipped cream to my lunch yesterday. All three ooohed with appreciation. Very gratifying.

Then, without blinking, I quickly popped a roast beef wrap in front of me. It was only three simple elements: roast beef, mustard, and a spinach wrap. It looked perfect.

I bit into it casually, as if I didn't really want to whoop it up because I'd managed to whip up something slightly complex. But as soon as I took the first bite, I regretted my showoff tendency. I'd wanted it to look as if I'd popped them simultaneously—which was a skill beyond my grasp at the moment. But I'd switched from chocolate cake to roast beef wrap so quickly, there'd been bleed through. Instead of mustard, I had chocolate icing. Surprisingly, roast beef and chocolate icing don't go together well. But I was just going to have to pretend it tasted like mustard. Yummy.

"You've been practicing." Samuel seemed most impressed, although all three of them smiled at me.

"Don't you?"

"Not really."

"Comes easy to you?" Yes, said my careful intelligence work (Maria was truly gabby at the pep rally). "You're lucky you don't have parents who didn't let you practice your magic."

All three of them looked shocked. "They didn't—"

"Mortals get freaky about stuff like that." I looked right into those eyes of his—which, speaking of freaky, the lenses of his glasses made his eyes seem to float outside his head when I looked that close.

"Right. What you need is a good study group—like we have." I could have kissed Samuel right then and there—if it wouldn't have given the entire lunchroom the wrong idea, never mind Samuel himself.

Maria and Denise nodded, and I was glad I had picked their table yesterday. It had been sheer luck—and a smidge of good instinct. They didn't say a word about me being in remedial magic classes. I felt a little twinge about using them. But I had a goal, and it wasn't hanging out at the geekoid table forever.

"I hadn't thought of that! Samuel, you're brilliant." Perhaps I shouldn't take advantage of being a cute teenage girl. But, hey, at the moment it's the best thing I've got going for me. "I wish I knew some people, but so far I've only met you guys. And you're way too advanced for me. Do you think Marlys Bledsoe might be a good choice?" In class this morning, Marlys had turned a rabbit—and herself— bright blue.

Samuel had perked up as the discussion veered away from death and into the realm of study groups and getting together outside of school. And I was sure it had nothing to do with the word "study." My casual mention of Marlys was just to nudge him over to the idea that I would be doing him a favor instead of vice versa.

"You have all this mortal stuff you could show us—we'd be lucky to have you." Done. He had now asked me to do him a favor and join his study group.

"Great! And you can come to dinner and meet my dad, then, too." My dad was the only really "mortal stuff" I could think of to show him, not that I'd let on. If I played it right, he'd never realize that what I wanted was to pick his brain and learn everything I hadn't learned in the last sixteen years in the shortest time possible. "Is Saturday good?"

"I can't," Maria said. "I have to go to my mom's wedding." I could tell she was disappointed, so I tried to look disappointed, too, despite the fact I really wanted Samuel alone—boys on their own are much easier to manage. If the girls were there, we might actually end up doing regular homework instead of the mega-fast-track tutoring I'd need to get out of remedial classes.

However, I'd obviously missed something, because the topic had shifted while I was doing an inward touchback. Both Samuel and Denise were staring at Maria as if she'd just announced she was the one getting married, not her mom. "*Who's* getting married?"

Maria blushed and whispered, "Mom is getting married again—but don't repeat that to anyone. She and her boyfriend are going to Vegas to elope."

Denise whistled. "Wow. I'm sorry for you."

"Is he a jerk?" I asked, trying to be sympathetic. I knew that game. I'd held the hand of all my friends as they dealt with all the changes in dads and moms. Everyone in my school had gone through it, it seemed, except me.

"No. She doesn't have the approval of the high council." Maria kept her voice low, and then shrugged as if she needed to apologize for her mother. "What can I say, she's two hundred years old and this is her fifth husband."

I couldn't really get into all the drama about eloping. Or even fifth husbands. "What's the big deal? People elope all the time. Life goes on."

They looked at me as if I were a baby going goo goo goo and drooling all over my bib. "The high council is supposed to approve all witch weddings," Denise explained. "They can get testy when it doesn't happen."

"Oh." I didn't really have anything to say about that, so I just listened to the rather horrible stories of what happened when the high council got angry (I started picturing twelve Agathas in a white room and gave myself a headache).

I confess I was glad when lunch was done and it was time to visit my lovely locker 666 and pretend to get something out of my backpack. Maybe a tissue this time, since I didn't need a tampon or lipstick.

I listened to the squeaks and slams of everyone else opening their lockers. It made me miss my old school, where we actually needed our lockers. Not that some people didn't treat them more like a second home than others.

In my old locker, I'd had a box of tissues and one of tampons, a sweater in case I got cold, and a cute little case of emergency makeup. Not to mention pictures of the team taped to my door so I could get a quick pick-me-up in between classes.

I was thinking about popping a picture of my boy into my locker when I realized it didn't really matter. The stupid lock—supposedly keyed to the touch of my finger—refused to open, no matter what I tried. I popped back into class tissue-less. It wasn't a big deal. I could always materialize one if I needed it. After all, it was good practice, and I needed plenty of that.

*

MADDIE: New look work on the Salemites?
ME: Im not a scud Yet
MADDIE: Ha Bet they think U rock

ME: As if! I want 2 come home Did Brent
make first string?
MADDIE: Of course
ME: Send pix?
MADDIE: On the way Send me some of
Salem hotties!
ME: Not 1 is clickworthy Boo hoo
MADDIE: Look harder

I changed the subject when Maddie asked me about hotties at my school. The question was getting annoying. Shouldn't my best friend get that I wasn't anywhere near ready to give up my hopes for a life—and boyfriend—in Beverly Hills? Why was she pushing me? Of course, she was probably just curious—and I was definitely afraid to let her see random pics of the kids at Agatha's. She'd know something was way weird if I did, the way even the kewl kids dressed at witch school. Sigh.

If only we could talk on the phone or e-mail. But, no. Her mother had grounded her sometime during the two weeks it had taken my family to make the trip to Salem. For what, Maddie hadn't said. But her mom was still so up and down from her divorce, it could have been because Maddie looked like her dad.

It would be a month before I could hear Maddie's voice. Life sucked. At least her mom had forgotten to ban text messaging (she'd never ban the cell phone for incoming—how would she make Maddie's life miserable if she couldn't reach her 24/7?). Which meant I'd have to face another day at Agatha's without a major gossip fest with Maddie.

In any new school, you feel like an alien newly landed on another planet for the first week (for some people the feeling lasts forever, but I trusted that wouldn't be true for me—I'm not completely clueless). I hadn't had too much sympathy for new kids before, but by the third day at Agatha's, I wondered if I needed to apologize to a couple of people.

I was finally getting used to being popped from class to class, and starting to get the hang of the second of transition that popping required. Even going to school hadn't been such a hardship (turns out getting lost in the locker room wasn't really my fault—Mom was supposed to pop me to the office that first day, but she didn't read the manual in time to know that, just like she forgot to give me the spell book).

Parents only have to pop you the first day. The rest of the time the students are supposed to home in on their lockers. I don't know what might happen if I couldn't concentrate on the locker—just because I was, say, thinking about Mr. Bindlebrot.

Fortunately, I hadn't popped into the boys' locker room again, though the thought had been so tempting, I worried that I might do it by accident, despite all the binding spells the school had in place to prevent such things.

And no wonder. The sight of Mr. Bindlebrot in a towel was definitely not on the approved Agatha curriculum. It was never going to leave me, I consoled myself, as I managed to make it to the main hallway, where once again I had to fight with the stupid locker 666 to get it to open. Maybe I'd have to bring in some oil for the hinges—or would Agatha's consider that contraband?

Apparently, according to the whispers and giggles, even in witchland a triple six was not a fortuitous number. And I'd gotten it on my very first try. Go figure. I thought about changing lockers, but instincts honed by eleven years of school told me that I'd need to build up my reputation before I did something so wimpy.

"Hey, 666 Girl!" Anonymous Boy was starting to get on my nerves. Big-time. I hated being the new girl, but 666 Girl seemed like a nickname that puts a Teflon coating on one of those steep, spirally slides at the kiddie playground. Straight down to loser land. Leave it to Anonymous Boy to gift me with a name based on something I couldn't help. Not to mention a nickname that would likely stick, because it was easy to say and I was new enough that only a very few people knew my real name. Sigh.

I turned, knowing that it is 100 percent loser to pretend you hate whatever inane nickname has been bestowed upon you by the gods-to-be. Not that Anonymous Boy was a true god-to-be, but it was clear he believed he was one, I thought, as I turned around.

As it happened, he was not a god-to-be. Nope. He was a full-fledged god himself. In a bad-boy way, with tousled hair and big brown eyes that said "I don't want to be here, and neither do you. Let's blow this Popsicle stand."

My stomach did one of those little flip-flops. Not a big one like with Mr. Bindlebrot and the towel. But close. "Hi."

No Longer Anonymous Boy smiled, revealing beautiful teeth with just a hint of sharp edge, and leaned in close. "Need help with the combination?"

"I should have brought some oil for this door." I wasn't going to let him know I had thought, for one second, that he was going to kiss me. "It's just a bit sticky."

"Haunted." His brown eyes were focused on me, and I knew he was pure trouble. If it weren't for the hallway of people watching us, I'd have turned and run. Maybe.

"Excuse me?"

"It's haunted. Hironymous Tuttle. He was the first to have the locker number and he was teased so much by the other dudes that he shut himself in the locker, refused to eat, and died there."

He was cute, but he was making fun of me, and that ran his hottie factor down to below zero. "Really?" I said in my most Hollywood dismissive voice. It was one thing to tease someone behind her back, but to her face?

"Really." He hit the locker once. "Hi, old buddy, open up for this nice girl, she's in remedial class and she's not up to handling your hijinks . . . yet."

Oh. So he hadn't been kidding about the ghost, then. "How do you—?"

He leaned in, clearly disinterested in whatever inane question I was about to ask. "Sorry about the eraser trick. Skin and Bones gets to me sometimes."

He apologized with his eyes just slightly narrowed, as if to up the sincerity factor, and my stomach did another quick flippity-flop. "Teachers. They haven't got a clue how annoying they can be. So you're . . ." How do you ask a cool boy with a pirate's earring in his left ear why he's in remedial spells? Simple. You don't. ". . . not fond of him either?"

The lock in my hand started spinning and snapped open. By itself.

Bad Boy, formerly known as Anonymous Boy, tapped the door in a mock salute. "Good deal, Hi. Behave yourself."

I didn't know if he had aimed the cautionary advice at me or at the ghost that haunted my locker, because the cutest boy in the school popped away without a fare-thee-well. Which, in his case, would probably have been a "See ya."

So Anonymously Bad Boy was a hottie. And I had a class with him. Suddenly remedial spells didn't seem as horrible as it had at first. Although I'd have to ask around about why someone with such familiarity with the ways of ghosts was still in remedial spells. Had he been raised by wolves? Or was he half mortal, like I was?

I didn't find out the answers to those questions in the morning class, but I did find out his name. Daniel. Daniel Murdoch. (No, I did *not* ask him. Mr. Phogg said it because Daniel at last perversely refused to answer to *boy*—not that I blame him in the least.)

Despite knowing that there was a grade-A hottie in class, I still wanted out very badly. So I did something I shouldn't have. I asked Mr. Phogg if I could talk to him after class. He nodded impatiently, which made me hold my breath until I was sure his white-haired head wasn't going to snap off his bony neck from the sharp force of that motion. At the end of class I wondered if he remembered—until he popped the rest of the class away and we were alone in the classroom.

Mr. Phogg leaned down. I think he meant to make himself friendly—or at least more approachable. Unfortunately, up close there was a cool wave of air from him, like he'd been in a refrigerator for about a hundred years and hadn't quite warmed up. "Are you feeling unable to handle the material, Miss Stewart? I could always put you back a grade—or even two, if you like."

Back a grade? Was he kidding? No. He wasn't. He looked

so grave, he could have been lying in a coffin. "Do you offer extra credit?"

Most teachers at my old school would have been weeping with pride that they'd brought out my ambitious side. But Mr. Phogg just lifted the heavy, wrinkled lids of his eyes a bit more—just enough that I could see his eyes were a milky white color. Yuck.

"I mean, I'm only in remedial spells because I was in the mortal realm for a long time. I want to do whatever I can to get into regular magic class ASAP." Yes, I was babbling. But it was his fault. Those eyes could turn The Rock into a babbler.

"Patience is a virtue, Miss Stewart."

No. Patience is my mom's name—and it's her fault I'm here in the first place. "I don't want to rush in a sloppy way," I assured him. "I just don't want to waste any time."

"Just like your mother was at your age, as I remember."

He waited for me to respond, but I didn't have a clue. At last I gave just the faintest giggle, hoping that if I'd guessed wrong, he'd think I was coughing instead of giggling.

He took it as a giggle. And he was not happy. "Not a good thing in my class, I warn you. Slow and steady is the way you want to go when you're a bit behind the curve." He laughed, a creepy laugh that sounded like the wind going through rusted metal. Kind of like the tape my dad played for our trick-or-treaters at Halloween.

"But–" I scrambled to think of a killer compliment, but all I could think of was that he knew my mom when she was my age. And I didn't think that was a point in my favor.

"Your regular homework will offer you sufficient growth and progress, Miss Stewart. And perhaps teach you the value of patience."

He waved his hand before I could open my mouth. It was annoying how dismissive the teachers at Agatha's could be– literally. Mr. Bindlebrot and the rest of the math class popped in before I could blink. So much for a little well-placed brownnosing.

Chapter 9

MADDIE: R U really gonna try out 4 their
team?
ME: If ur mom decided to move U across the
country wouldnt you?
MADDIE: I guess Thank goodness her custody
agreement w Dad wont let her
ME: Lucky
MADDIE: Maybe U should convince ur dad 2
divorce ur mom and move back
ME: As if! Hez so stuck on her its gaggin
MADDIE: OK If ur parents arent coming 2
their senses I guess U dont have ne choice
Good luck

ME: Thx I need it

MADDIE: Noway U R captain quality

ME: In Beverly Hills Not here

MADDIE: U better not be sayin they R better than us

ME: Noway Maybe Ive just lost it already

MADDIE: U need a big scoop of Rocky Road

ME: I need a tractor scoop of it! If no team I dunno know what 2 do Maybe join chess club

MADDIE: Id have to come kidnap U if U went all chess on me

ME: Please!

*

"Take this liquid of life I hold,
And tinge it with berries so sweet
That drink it children beg so bold
And crave to taste it with tongues so fleet."

Okay. So there's a reason I'm in remedial summoning and spells. I admit it—but I don't have to like it.

Four hours of homework practice it took me to turn water into strawberry iced tea. I'd got the iced tea part straight off, but for some reason I kept getting grape instead of strawberry. Since I intended to show Skin and Bones I could do anything and everything he asked, it was important to get it right.

Just when I thought I wasn't ever going to manage it—I was so desperate that I almost asked Dorklock for help—I changed one word in the spell and got strawberry iced tea, perfectly sugared. Who'd have thought that substituting berries for fruit would have made that much difference? Someone not in remedial magic class, I guess.

"Lights out, Prudence." Mom stuck her head in the door, even though she could have just projected her voice into my room with magic. She saw the glass of iced tea on the table and asked, "Need any help with your home-work?"

"Nope. All done." I drank the iced tea. Yuck. Too sweet. "Mr. Phogg seems to think you should have been called Impatience, not Patience, when you were young."

"He said that? Out of the blue?" Mom always asked the right questions. Usually I hated that. But this time I'd counted on it.

"I asked about extra credit and he tried to get me to go back to ninth-grade magic classes!" I hoped the juxtaposi-tion of my two comments would serve to tickle her moth-erly guilt. Maybe Mr. Phogg wouldn't have had it in for me if it wasn't for Mom. Maybe.

She frowned for a minute, as if she'd tasted something bit-ter. But then she put on the false-cheer smile moms are so good at. "Mr. Phogg can be a bit methodical, Prudence, but there's no one better to learn spells and summoning from."

I could think of at least three. In order, from least horrible to most: Samuel, Mom, and Dorklock. I wish I could
think of a spell that would make sure the studying with
Samuel would pay off quickly enough that I wouldn't need
to resort to the next two options. Because time and space
are converging, and a place on the team—and in the school—
are on the line.

I'd nearly had a heart attack when I finally read the rules
on the postcard that appeared when I signed up for cheerleading tryouts. It was only dumb luck that had made me
look at them at all. After all, I'd been a cheerleader—and a
very good one, according to all my coaches—since sixth
grade. But here in the witch realm, everything was just a
little bit different. Including the rules and regulations for
cheerleading tryouts.

They hadn't made sense at first read: no flying over ten
miles per hour, no turning the opposition into toads during a toss, and no double spell casting (apparently it has
a great effect when it works, but leaves a big mess when
it doesn't—and it only works about 10 percent of the
time).

A little research at the school library told me all I needed
to know—theoretically. Definitely not the way I want to
make my splash—unless it looked like I wasn't going to
make the team, of course.

But I figured that was unlikely. If I could make the

team at Beverly Hills High, where even the second stringers had had a nose job, a boob job, and spent the afternoons with a personal trainer, I should be able to manage here, where most of the cheerleaders had a little extra padding that suggested they didn't work out as much as they should.

Tryouts were in the girls' gym. I wasn't sure what the girls would be wearing (sounds silly, but cheerleaders are made or broken by what they wear even more than how they look—all those fancy moves mean nothing if the people in the stands can't see how the body moves). So I covertly eavesdropped on the cheerleaders' table at lunch, in hopes of overhearing something that would give me an edge, but all I heard about was how the complexion-clearing spells could be overused to the point of turning skin to alligator.

So when school was over and the girls' locker room doors appeared in the hallway, I held back. Normally, I like to be first in line, but this time I decided to take a peek and see what the other girls were wearing so I could zap a rad outfit for myself before I committed to the gym and the scrutiny of all the others.

To my relief, it seemed to be general cheerleading prac-tice type stuff—shorts, belly shirts, sneakers in a rainbow of colors. I popped myself into my blue shorts and green belly shirt. Just to stand out, I changed the color of my sneakers to match my shirt and turned the laces the same blue as my shorts.

And then I went in to face the greatest challenge any high school junior ever faces: the cheerleading triumvirate–coach, last year's head cheerleader, and this year's head cheerleader.

The funny thing was that I had the potential to be a hottie here (I'm not bragging, just the facts). Back home, I'd been okay in the looks department, but nothing to break out the cameras for. I'd even been worried I'd be cut from the team when Dad refused to let me have any work done, but fortunately, I was a good flyer (no one knew I was really flying) and, after Katie Williams landed on her fake boobs and they burst, I got top spot.

So, instead of work, I had a few magic tricks that let me compensate for the times when my support faltered, or didn't have the muscle to throw me high enough in the air. As Mandy, the head cheerleader my freshman year, said to anyone who dared to sneer at her "improvements"–"Some of us are blessed by nature, and some of us are blessed by American Express. However you got it, honey, make the most of it." (I think she stole that line from someone else, but she sure made it her own. I heard a rumor that she'd had it engraved on her cell phone. Normally I didn't believe outrageous rumors, even in Beverly Hills, where a lot of them were true. This one, I thought was highly possible.)

Basically, I figured since I'd already been using witchcraft secretly to help my cheerleading, it would be a small adjustment to use it openly.

I know, I know. The fact I was in remedial spells should have been a clue. But what can I say? I've always been a witch in the mortal world. Kind of like the seeing man in the land of the blind that my dad loves to lecture about. Now I was more like Mr. Magoo in a world of people with x-ray vision. Sucks. Big-time.

But hey, I'm not one to complain unless I think it will get me my way. So I kept my fingers crossed that my learning curve would be more like a straight line up.

The tryouts were not very different from back home . . . at first. I didn't stand out too much. Sure, everyone knew I was the half mortal, but they'd started getting used to it. Hardly anybody stared openly anymore. It wasn't like I had horns, and the wardrobe changes helped me blend in with all the kids who had better things to do than worry about what the half-mortal reject was up to.

Coach Gertie, a witch with flyaway red hair and a strong Irish brogue, had a whistle, which was annoying in a normal, mortal way. Coach Riley had been so addicted to hers back in Beverly Hills that someone once tested it for crack cocaine as a joke.

Another familiar thing was the way Coach Gertie put us through our paces: Ready Position, Buckets, High V, K motion, Spankies, L motion. For the first time since I'd been forced to start a whole new life, I felt like I knew what I was doing in Salem. It was my time to show Coach I could snap out the sharpest moves on the team.

But it quickly became clear that my standards were higher than the coach's. At first, I just thought everyone was rusty after a summer off. The floor moves were sloppy, to say the least. The best V's looked like U's, and the rest looked like they were being arrested by the fashion police.

Back home, these girls wouldn't have had a chance at JV, but Agatha's was a small school and evidently Coach Gertie wasn't a stickler like Coach Riley had been. Of course, Riley'd had nothing on our last year's head cheerleader, who'd made us practice in the mirror until we could do the moves right in our sleep. Agatha's head cheerleader, a bleached blonde named Tara, looked the part . . . as long as she was standing still. And then she looked like she needed sleep—or lots of high-octane coffee. Worse, she looked like that while she was trying to lead us in our tryout moves. Not a good sign for the regional competitions, never mind me showing up Chezzie at Nationals. Bummer.

I snapped out my moves, tried not to collide with the girls on either side of me, and put on my innocent cheerleader smile while I asked some questions to try to figure out why all the girls—even the seniors—were so lax about floor moves.

When the girl on my left (one of the girls whose V looked like she was being arrested) smacked me with an untidily extended arm, I took the opportunity to catch her eye. "Which cheerleading camp did you go to this summer?"

"Are you kidding? My mom's really into snorkeling, so we went to the Seychelles for the whole summer. If I never see another piece of coral again for my whole life, I won't mind."

Unfortunately, Tara overheard my question and flew over to us (literally). "No talking, girls. Concentrate on those moves." She was looking at me, like I wasn't letter perfect. As if.

The girl I'd tried to turn into an ally shouted out, "Hey Tara, did you know they have cheerleader camps in the mortal realm?"

"Of course they do," she sneered, as if cheerleader camps were where mortals went to die. "If you can't fly, you have to practice harder."

Everyone laughed. Okay. So that was one answer as to why these girls didn't take floor moves seriously. Camp really helps you focus. And there was no focus on this floor, unless it was in the little "pick me" spells the wannabes were whispering under their breath.

I'm not trying to be immodest, but really. I was the only one who could snap a tight set of moves. And timing. Everyone seemed to have their own beat going in their

heads—not the best way to get in synch for killer move-
ment.

Coach clapped her hands loudly at the end of the two-
hour tryouts. "Great job, girls." I could see she really meant
it. She thought those sloppy moves were fine. "I'll see you
again Monday for the second half of tryouts. Make sure
your parents sign the permission slip for me to remove your
binding spells, or you'll be disqualified. I don't have time to
track parents down all over the world."

Another thing I was beginning to understand was that
witch parents are really a lot like the rich parents of my for-
mer classmates. Lots of time spent pursuing fun and special
interests. But at the same time, witch parents are seriously
more protective of their kids. They never leave them alone
without a bunch of protective and/or binding spells. Mega
annoying. It was bad enough back home when we had the
"always charged and ready rule": cell phones nearby and
turned on so our parents could hear our happy voices and
know we were okay at random moments of their choosing.
Here in the land of witches who could fly, read minds, cast
spells, and transubstantiate, alarms were always going off
because some parent had set their antismoking spell so ultra
sensitive that it went off when the Bunsen burner was
turned on in chem lab.

I'd asked Samuel about this after two days of jumping at
the ear-shattering whine that seemed to come from nowhere

at the worst times. "What's with the alarms? Do witches have a big weapons-to-school problem?"

He shrugged, obviously used to it. "Don't mortal parents put restrictions on their kids? You know, curfew, and grounding, all those metal detectors? And speaking of metal detectors, does it hurt to go through one?"

"No. It doesn't hurt to go through a metal detector any more than it hurts to walk through a door," I said patiently. "Besides, those restrictions don't mean anything as long as you don't get caught."

"How can you not get caught?" There was more than shock on his face—there was a definite layer of curiosity. Well, well, well. Geekoid Samuel had a little taste for the bad-boy rep. Whodathunkit?

"Take curfew. If you set the clocks back a little, you can give yourself an extra twenty or thirty minutes past the time the 'rents want you home. Unless they notice, you're set. And if they do notice, you can always plead you set your watch by their clocks. And grounding— nobody ever puts up with grounding. That's what windows were made for—leaving the house and getting back in undetected."

Samuel was sensitive about my criticism, I found, when he began to defend 'rents and restrictions. "Well, mortal kids can only get into car wrecks or burn down a house. Witch kids . . . remember Chernobyl?"

"Are you telling me a Russian nuclear power plant went melty because of a witch?" I asked, horrified.

Samuel nodded. "A witch kid who was manifesting a major Water Talent. His parents had been studying the climate changes of Siberia through the years, forgot to put a protective spell on him, and voilà, he got mad and–accidentally–boiled the water from the core. The council had to make it seem like the humans had done it by being careless, because not even a turn-back-time spell could fix that disaster."

Denise nodded, a French fry dangling from her lips. "That was quite a meltdown. My parents double charmed me from then on."

Great. And I just happened to live with the Dorklock, who was going to manifest his Talent in as annoying a way as possible if his past history was anything to judge by. No wonder Mom had convinced Dad to move here. "Jeez. And I thought having a party for two hundred of your closest friends when your parents were out of town was a silly idea."

"We have a few more restrictions than mortal teens," Samuel agreed. "But when you consider that most of our parents have spent centuries seeing what kind of trouble they can get into, it makes sense that they'd want to protect us from the worst of our mistakes for a while."

"Even grown witches don't always know when to avoid trouble," Maria had chimed in.

"Don't worry, Maria. Your mom's still young. They'll go easy on her." Denise, ever sympathetic, patted her hand and popped a big square of chocolate next to Maria's half-eaten hot pastrami sandwich.

"She never learns. She always thinks this husband is the right one. She's almost two hundred!" Maria took a big bite of chocolate, and two tears made tracks to her chin.

"Love makes us all crazy, mortal and witch," I offered, not knowing what else to say. Maria's mother had been summoned to the high council for her unauthorized wedding. Nobody knew what was going to happen to her. "Look at my mom. She married a mortal and lived in L.A. for twenty years with practically no magic."

Maria was much more heartened by that than I would have been. But then, she knew something I didn't. "Thanks for reminding me. Your mom survived a visit to the council for her unauthorized wedding, so I guess mine can too."

My mom survived a visit to the council? I churned those words for a few minutes. Why hadn't I known that? Even Grandmama never threw that at Dad when she complained about his fuddy-duddy mortal ways. It couldn't have been that bad, though, could it? Because no one ever talked about it at our house.

By the time I got back to the conversation at hand, Samuel was saying, "I mean, think about it. Mortals live, what, seventy or eighty years? And they think twenty-five is young. So your mom is only a teenager in witch terms."

Grandmama was coy about admitting to anything above five hundred, but she'd dropped enough hints that I knew she was much older. The sheer horror of what Samuel was saying hit me. "If two hundred is a teenager, what's sixteen? A rugrat?"

All three looked at me blankly for a minute, but no one seemed to have an answer.

Another question, more horrific, spurted out. "Is twenty-one the age of the majority for witches, like it is for mortals? Or do we have to wait hundreds of years to become adults?"

Samuel laughed, finally getting where I was coming from (probably because he was a mortal groupie). "Adulthood for witches isn't an age. It's a test."

"A test?" Great. Yet another place my lack of witch training was sure to pay off big-time. Thanks, Mom.

"Yep." He seemed puzzled that I didn't already know this, but he didn't make fun of me for asking. "The Wisdom Test. Didn't your mom tell you about it?"

"No. She did not." And suddenly I was highly annoyed with my mother, who had dragged us here, dumped us into witch school, and still wasn't willing to tell us what we needed to know. Talent. Wisdom. What else didn't I know about? And then I had a truly terrible thought. Maybe, because I hadn't manifested my Talent yet, Mom was playing it down because I was the equivalent of not-too-swift in witchcraft. "How hard is this Wisdom Test?"

Denise shrugged. "My mom and dad passed it young, probably fifty-four. My grandmother gets teased by my grandfather, though. It took her twenty tries and she didn't pass until she was nearly a hundred."

Maria turned to Samuel. "Wasn't your mom the youngest ever to pass—on the first try, too?"

There was an awkward little pause at the mention of his mother, but Samuel tried to cover it with a big fake smile. "Yes. She was only twenty-four. But she was a really excellent witch."

"The best," Maria and Denise said together, with a little head bob of respect.

I bobbed with them, even though I didn't know anything about Samuel's mom. "Wow. It must be a hard test." And how likely was it that Dorklock and I would pass it easily when we'd been denied—and were still being denied—access to some really simple facts. Like the fact we had to pass a Wisdom Test in the first place? Or that our mom had defied the high council to marry our dad? What other big stuff didn't I know that was going to come back to bite me?

Samuel's fake smile had morphed to a real one as we talked. "I suppose it's like any test. You just need to be prepared. My dad says you mostly have to use common sense."

Denise snorted. "Granny Anna says they ask trick questions to trip you up."

"Trick questions. Great. Just what I need," I sighed.

"It's not as big a deal as you think, Pru. Chill." Samuel's smile was completely real this time. Okay. If my utter terror could be used to make him laugh, I could live with that.

Maria said kindly, "You could always live in the mortal realm until you're considered an adult in the witch realm. It's fairly common in the time between figuring out how to counter your parents' protective spells and passing the Wisdom Test."

Aha. Yet another interesting fact I probably would have learned in kindergarten if I'd been raised in the witch realm. At least I could be grateful that being a witch wasn't going to interfere with my college plans. I'd had enough life-plan disruptions for the moment. "So the binding spells can be countered?"

"Of course. It just takes skill," Maria said, with such confidence that I wondered if she'd already found a way around at least one. "Like when mortal kids beat getting grounded by going out the window. Although, the kids with a Magic Talent have a big edge."

"Well, then . . ." I flashed my pearly whites directly at Samuel. "I'm glad you're going to help me study my way out of remedial classes. Maybe it will help me uncover my hidden Magic Talent and pass the Wisdom Test just a few decades earlier." Or maybe I wouldn't manifest any Talent at all and would get kicked out of witch school. Would Mom let me go live with Maddie then? It was an idea to consider, even though I didn't like the thought of losing at anything.

And maybe I'd consider asking Daniel—who clearly knew how to get around a lot of binding spells—to show me how to get out of class every so often. After all, no kid, witch or mortal, should be expected to survive high school without playing hooky every now and then.

Chapter 10

ME: So what position R U this year?

MADDIE: Tryouts 1st please We all have 2 wait 2 find out whoz gonna be HC

ME: Not Chezzie?

MADDIE: Not yet Its drivin her crazy She thought she was a lock

ME: She probably is U know

MADDIE: Well I can hope as long as coach keeps us on the hook

ME: Heres wishin us both gr8 places on our teams

MADDIE: Wouldnt it be weird if we meet at nationals?

ME: No fear My school doesnt enter
competitions
MADDIE: U can change that!
ME: Let me make the team be4 U have me
whippin it into shape!
MADDIE: K

I was secretly glad that Coach was making Chezzie wait
to take my spot as head cheerleader. Not that I didn't think
she would get it. Just like I was sure some girl was going to
catch Brent's eye. But I could dream as long as neither one
had actually happened yet. Dream that Mom would stop
this horrible experiment and take us home.

Still, I'm a practical girl. Dreams aside, I needed to move
ahead on my plan to take Agatha's by storm. Samuel's
arrival on Saturday was met with all the embarrassing attention that my family was capable of giving. The only piece of
good luck was that Grandmama didn't pop in for a visit to
pinch his cheeks and tell him how adorable he was.

Mom got more about Samuel's family lineage out of him
than his family probably knew he knew (although nothing
about how his mother died, which I really wanted to know).
She did it with a smile, and I know he was dazzled, not
intimidated, by her interrogation. Typical Mom.

Dad shook his hand and clapped his shoulder in a greeting that went out in the fifties. "Nice to see that Prudence

is making friends. She was a little worried that she'd be a pariah here." Great, Dad! Why don't you tell him about the zit I put a pound of cover-up on ten minutes ago!

He also warned us that we needed to study and that, though my mom had lifted the binding spell that made hives appear if I was alone with a boy, she had replaced it with a warning whistle. "Just keep your hands to yourself, son, and there won't be any need to cover your ears and run for the hills." My father is so subtle. Not.

We worked hard, don't get me wrong. I'm not a slacker. Summoning. Simple spells. Even simple levitation, which was why I was going to be big-time bruised in the morning. But there comes a time when your brain needs rest. Like after a stressful dinner with nosy parents and a bratty little brother.

For some reason, rest (and work, and breathing) made my mind turn to Daniel. I debated for at least ten minutes whether to ask Samuel about him. But I was so curious that I knew if I didn't ask Samuel now, I might do something horrendous—like ask one of the cheerleaders at the tryouts on Monday. Kiss of death to any rep I wanted to develop if I let on to the wrong girl I was interested in bad-boy Daniel.

Everyone thinks cheerleaders are cute perky chicks who live for positive affirmation in rhyme. But the sport (and it *is* a sport) is cutthroat when it comes to two things: competitions and hooking up with boys.

"Hey, I found out who was dissing me at lunch last week.

It was Daniel Murdoch." I tried to keep it light for two reasons: I don't like anyone else knowing my business; and I didn't want my new tutor getting jealous. It could seriously cut into our study time.

"What a surprise." Samuel scowled. "He's bad news."

"Well, I kinda guessed that when he sent the erasers at my face on the first day of remedial summoning and spells. Speaking of which—why is he in a remedial magic class?"

"Even though his Magic Talent manifested early, he always tries shortcuts and the dangerous things we're supposed to learn when we're older. But his spell work is clumsy beyond belief."

"As is mine!" I reminded him, offended on both my own and Daniel's part.

"But you have an excuse. Your mom didn't encourage your skills because she wanted you to fit in."

"And because it gave my dad the heebie-jeebies," I added.

"Your dad's a mortal. Daniel comes from a great family, master witches and warlocks all of them. And what did he do? He ran away when he was thirteen. Didn't come home for two years."

Ran away? "I didn't know witches could do that." One of the girls in my class in Beverly Hills ran away in eighth grade. Her mom and dad freaked. There were posters everywhere. The police even interviewed our class. They found her six months later in New York City. But she never came back to school with us. I heard her parents sent her to some fancy private school that did double time as a kiddie prison. She was a weird chick, always going on about horoscopes and how she could talk to horses. But she seemed nice enough, and she always gave me the nuts off her brownie because she didn't like them.

"His Magic Talent is really awesome," Samuel explained. "He's like a magic version of a hacker. When he ran away, his parents really freaked. He broke twenty binding spells, and none of their locating spells worked. They hired someone to cast a repeating loop of spells, and he still didn't get caught until he was sick with the flu one day and couldn't ward off one of the locating spells in the repeating loop."

"Then he sure doesn't sound like he belongs in remedial magic." I wondered if he'd be interested in tutoring. But, no, a guy like that is not to be counted on. I needed someone steady, like Samuel.

"They should have kicked him out of Agatha's altogether," Samuel said, shaking his head.

"He's just not the kind to like rules. What's the big deal?"

"That's like saying a Rip Van Winkle spell will get you a good nap. Ever since Daniel came home, he doesn't listen to anyone's rules. He pops in and out of class halfway through, and he"—Samuel's voice squeaked, which made him blush as he finished—"laughs through detention."

I didn't like Daniel being dissed. Don't ask me why. Insanity inherited from my mother (who married a mortal, after all). "Well, I guess he must be used to it after so many years of doing the big D. I knew kids like that."

He sighed like a parent who's just dug the straight-F report card out of the trash. "Our detention isn't anything like the one at your mortal school."

"Why? What do they do—hang you upside down from the ceiling like a bat?"

"Only if you're really bad, and do something like set off a level-five spell without supervision. Which Daniel has done twice, I might add."

This was a little more than I wanted to hear. But, still . . . "So what do they do in regular detention?"

"They sink you up to your neck in liquid quicksand. You can't move for the whole hour. It's horrible."

"You . . . ?" Again, the barrier of not being able to ask a loser question popped up to silence me. But then I remembered this was Samuel. He had a crush on me, and a very soft heart, too. Curiosity could reign supreme. "When were you in detention?"

There was just a little hitch in his breath, and he fiddled with his glasses before he answered. "Only once. When I was in seventh grade."

I probably shouldn't have tortured him—his cheeks and chin were flushed, and he wasn't looking at me. But hey,

I wanted to know, and I was pretty sure he would tell me if I asked. "What did you do?"

"I popped into the girls' locker room," he said sheepishly.

Foolishly, I had taken a sip of my soda after asking, so naturally I choked on it and spent a minute or two coughing like a barking seal before I could deal with that surprising answer. "You're a perv?"

"It was an accident," Samuel insisted.

"Seventh-grade boy. Girls' locker room. Sure it was." Okay, so I don't take surprises well. Sue me for being the queen of mean.

"No, really." He was red up to his hairline. "It was just, I was thinking about what would happen if I did it—I wasn't thinking about doing it, just what if, and . . ."

"I get it." No more throwing stone from this glass house. I hadn't meant to catch Mr. Bindlebrot in a towel, but I had. "I still pop into the wrong place from time to time myself." And get some interesting views, just like Samuel. "So, was it worth detention?"

He flashed me a dimple. "Visions for a lifetime."

Well, well, well. Maybe Samuel *does* have a mischievous streak after all. "I guess you and Daniel have more in common than you know."

Mentioning Daniel cooled the room by about a hundred degrees. "Stay away from Daniel. He's bad news."

I shrugged. "He got Hi to open up for me."

"He did?" Despite the scowl, I think Samuel was impressed.

"Yes. He did. When no one else," I said pointedly, and he suddenly got very interested in looking deep into his soda can, "had the common decency to warn me my locker was haunted."

He didn't look up from the depths of his soda, but he did mumble an apology. "I didn't think you'd believe me."

"What?" I hadn't been sure Samuel had even known about Hi. Until now. The rat.

"You're still a little . . ." He stared at me as if he was trying to put an image too big for words directly into my brain.

But I was clueless. "A little what?" Unhappy that he could have told me how to get into my locker any number of times? Darn right I was.

And then his meaning crushed in on me. "Mortal? Do you mean I'm still living like I did in the mortal world?" Low blow. "I see ghosts all the time. There are some in this house! What about Goody Deering—she greeted you at the door. Didn't you see her pat my cheek?"

He held up his hands as if to push my growing rage away. "It takes time to adjust. There's nothing wrong—"

For a minute I almost flipped out. Almost. But I needed him to help me get out of remedial spells. So all I did was levitate like we'd practiced all afternoon. Straight to the ceiling. "Good. Then if there's nothing wrong with me, I guess you won't mind coming back to help me study again tomorrow."

"I can't come tomorrow, but I can come Monday." He said it so fast, I knew he was way into me—even when he knew my mom wasn't ever going to let him get close enough to kiss me.

"Great." I smiled like all was forgiven. After all, he hadn't once mentioned asking Maria and Denise to join us. I'd expected to have to explain how I was too shy to look stupid in front of so many people.

Probably lightning should have struck me then and there for being so mean to him. But it didn't. "I have final tryouts Monday. Come Tuesday. You can stay for dinner again."

I didn't have much time to celebrate Dad's yes to the Mercedes. Well, to a car. He'd downsized me from a Mercedes to a Jetta between the orange juice and the pancakes at breakfast on Monday morning.

I swallowed the bite of pancake I'd just taken and checked that my hearing hadn't gone out on me overnight (Dad kept saying it would if I didn't turn down the volume on my tunes). "You want me to get a job?"

"Calm down. You have experience as a babysitter, and you could always—"

"Babysitting? Don't you want me to do well in school? Not to mention all the practice it takes to be a good cheerleader." If I made the cut at tryouts today, which didn't bear thinking about while I was eating breakfast.

"A mortal car requires mortal insurance and mortal gas. In order to pay for them, you have to earn money."

"Mom?" I thought she would help. "Can't I just zap a policeman if he stops me? Put a spell on the car so it looks registered?"

"No." Mom was not going to be supportive. "If you have a mortal car, using mortal streets, you need to pay for the privilege."

"But—"

"No buts, young lady."

"Why do you need a car?" Dorklock, as usual, was clueless. "You can zap yourself anywhere you want to go."

"You wouldn't understand, you're just a kid." The gifted-and-talented program was probably wasted on him. But I didn't say so because it might make Dad mad enough to take the car back. Besides, the little brat had been learning to zap himself through time and space while I was stuck learning to move erasers one by one.

I tried one more round of mega-guilt. Last chance, all guns ablaze. "I wouldn't have this problem if you hadn't moved us here."

I think Dad was almost ready to give in, but Mom wasn't so easy. "Nice try, but it won't work. If you want the car, you earn the money."

"How much does it cost?"

Dad, happy to be useful, leaped onto the Internet, made a quick phone call to his car insurance agent, and handed me the bad news just before it was time to pop out for school.

Looked like I'd be babysitting twenty-four hours a day if I wanted the car. "Deal. But can you pay the first month's payment as an early birthday present?"

Dad said yes before Mom could object. Now I just had to find babysitting gigs for children who liked to sleep, read, and play Barbies by themselves. Maybe I could learn to cast naptime spells.

I had plenty of time to earn enough to keep the car. Grandmama would be proud of my haggling abilities. Now all I had to do was figure out how to use the car to boost me out of new-girl status into kewl-girl status.

The problem with going to a witch school is that you pop in and out. No parking lot to show off your rad ride. No driver's ed class. Bringing up the subject wasn't as easy as I had hoped.

I'd thought Daniel might understand, but he wasn't in class when I popped into remedial summoning and spells. Disappointing. I had rehearsed thanking him for his help with Hi. I also wanted to quietly brag that I'd found out Hi enjoyed brownies. A brownie a day for easy access to my locker (666 or not) seemed like a small price to pay to an oversensitive ghost.

About halfway into learning how to find a simple rhyme to improve our spells, Mr. Phogg aimed a Skeletor glare at a spot behind me. "Nice of you to accommodate the last half of my class in your busy schedule." He held out his bony hand. "Your pass?"

"Must have lost it." Daniel shrugged. I never would have thought you could hear a shrug, but I heard his, even though I didn't dare risk Skin and Bone's wrath by turning around to give him an encouraging smile. Not even when an eraser came out of nowhere and landed on my shoulder.

Turning around in Mr. Phogg's class earned you a demerit. Ten demerits meant you got a full grade lower on that month's work. I would simply die if I failed remedial magic.

It's funny, but I never would have guessed that remedial classes would be harder than the gifted classes. But they are. Loads. Instead of going for the big picture of how to create a great spell, we recited general spells over and over until we sounded like an overgrown kindergarten class reciting a mega-weird alphabet. We even had a big, old-fashioned chalkboard. Mr. Phogg didn't actually touch the chalk, he just kind of waved at it and it started writing spells and incantations on the board.

"Lost it," said Mr. Phogg dryly. "How unfortunate for you. Two weeks' detention."

There was a gasp in the classroom, and everyone (except me) looked at Daniel. Who shrugged again as Mr. Phogg recorded a storm of demerits. (No, I didn't turn around. I heard him shrug, I swear!)

In the hallway, just before lunch, there was a lot of murmuring that had Daniel's name drifting along in it. I ignored the gossip as I bribed Hi with more brownies and he spun my lock open for me.

I tried desperately not to picture Daniel buried in a vat of mud for two weeks straight after school. That thought alone made me feel like I couldn't breathe. I wondered if he'd run away again. I know I would if I were facing two weeks' detention at Agatha's.

A sudden hush in the hallway was my only warning before Daniel's hand came to rest on my locker door. "Glad to see you're treating my girl well, Hi."

My girl? A little presumptuous, but who was I to argue? "Hi and I have reached an agreement—free-and-clear access to the locker in exchange for an unlimited supply of brownies."

"Always pays to bribe the ghost, 666 Girl."

I almost didn't hate the nickname when he said it this time. "Skin and Bones likes to torment you, doesn't he?"

He grinned, as if two weeks of detention were two weeks on the beach. Which I guess they were, in a way, given how cold Massachusetts was even though it was only early fall.

"Why do you provoke him?" I asked. I genuinely wanted to know.

Daniel shrugged. "It's fun. Almost as much as sneaking out of class to play hooky."

There wasn't much to say about that. Even a pebble-strewn beach and a forty-degree wind gust were better than remedial spells.

"I hear you know a bit about playing hooky the mortal way."

"Me? I'm not a detention-type girl, myself." Especially with tryouts this afternoon and making the team on the line. Who had blabbed? Couldn't have been Samuel, since he'd practically growled whenever he'd said Daniel's name. Probably Denise or Maria.

"I'm going to skip all of next class. Want to come with and see how we do it here in the magic realm?"

My heart felt like it was about to pound out of my chest as I thought of detentions in vats of quicksand and the grounding of all groundings. Come with? Yes . . . except. My heart went from pound-pound-pound to full stop in one beat. We'd be alone together if I went with him. Alone. With my mom's triple-strength protective spells binding me.

"I have to go." And go I did, right into the safety of the crowded lunchroom. Leaving Daniel with a look of surprise on his face that still didn't erase his hottie looks.

Chapter 11

MADDIE: Chezzie made HC U were robbed

ME: Well I cant lead cheers a continent away
Did she sleep with coach?

MADDIE: Tee hee Nope lost 25 lbs and her
dad bought the uniforms

ME: Oh The usual way HC gets filled in BH

MADDIE: U got it

ME: I find out Monday if I made the team

MADDIE: Head?

ME: Noway! New girl here Ill be lucky if I
make it at all

MADDIE: The new uniforms are cheap Coach
is mad Were buyin jock itch powder

ME: Tell Chezzie 2 show her dad her rash
Maybe he will spring 4 a vat of powder
MADDIE: Id rather tell SuSu If her dad gets
the powder Coach will make her HC If he
buys new uniforms she makes her Queen of
the Cheerleaders
ME: U plannin 2 be a princess?
MADDIE: Im her best friend
ME: U are?
MADDIE: After U of course

I was determined to ignore the little click that went off in my head at the news that Coach had finally named Chezzie head cheerleader. It was like a lock had been set on my old life and I didn't have the combination to reopen it. Before, I could daydream about Mom and Dad coming to their senses and bringing us back home. I would show up at practice and reclaim my place as leader, natch. Maddie would hug me. Coach would have a tear glistening in her eye behind her wire-rims.

Now that Chezzie was officially head cheerleader, going back would be . . . interesting. To be fair, I'd probably have to wait until senior year to get named head cheerleader again. Which would mean pretending to think Chezzie knew what she was talking about when it came to a good cheer routine.

I could do it, though. I knew I could. I'd survived—so far—at Agatha's, hadn't I? If only Mom and Dad would come to their senses.

I was glad that Maddie had been willing to really chat. For a while her texts had been so short that I thought maybe she had back-burnered me. Except for the best-friend comment, this was the most normal our texts had been since I'd moved. I'm counting the days until her grounding is over and I can call her again.

Still, she couldn't know what it meant for me to make the team. She probably thought it should have been a done deal before I walked into the tryouts. But I couldn't explain the differences between witch tryouts and mortal tryouts to her. I'm not even sure that I knew all of them. Yet.

While I knew I didn't have a shot at head cheerleader, I'd been fairly confident that second tryouts would leave me with a place on the squad. That is, until Coach Gertie finished putting us through our floor warm-up with an ear-blasting set of whistles and said, "Okay. Preliminaries over with the mortal routines we worked on last time. Let's get to the good stuff, girls."

The mood in the room picked up. Everyone smiled, even the teensy girl with the ice pack on her chin.

"Follow Tara's lead, one at a time."

I confess, I hadn't been too impressed with Tara's floor

moves at the last tryouts. She really didn't seem to think sync mattered. But when Coach pointed to Tara, and she began to rise into the air while making the same movements we'd all just done on the ground, I had to give her cred. In the air, the sloppiness wasn't quite as noticeable. And there were a lot more ways to wow the crowd in the air.

Tara's big finale was putting both hands over her head and somersaulting backward, coming to a tiptoe touch-down on the ground. Great. Midair gymnastics. Not my specialty.

I stood about midway through the line and tried franti-cally to calm myself as I watched girl after girl do this move. It must be pretty simple, if everyone could do it. One thing I knew about cheerleading was that it was like every other sport: You weeded the great from the merely good by push-ing the limits until you had more failures than successes. Frappiola.

Coach pointed to me. I raised myself into the air and began sweating from the effort of moving through my rou-tine with no floor to support me. When my hands went up and I flipped backward, I smacked down on the ground. Hard.

Everyone laughed. For a moment I thought I was doomed to be a scud forever. I tried to make a rep-saving joke. "Wow, I'm glad I didn't try that move at the Nationals last year or Beverly Hills High would never have won."

You'd have thought I'd stuck an electrical cord up Coach's sweater. "Right, Miss . . . Stewart. Of course. I had forgotten that you were on a mortal team."

Tara said, "Mortal moves aren't enough here, though. Sorreee. Maybe after you figure out what your Talent is . . . if you have one . . . and you're out of remedial classes—"

Coach interrupted her. "Now, now, Tara. Let's not be hasty. That was a little rusty, Miss Stewart. That's to be expected since you've been at a mortal school. But if you've competed at Nationals, I'm sure . . . Why don't you try again."

Tara's frozen smile was cheerleader perfect, but I could read the frown beneath it. Big deal. I wasn't going to blow this chance just because the head cheerleader hated me.

Now that I knew what to expect, I managed to do it again without smacking into the floor. Granted, I was slower than some of the others, but I landed gracefully on my feet, in the right position and with the all-important smile on my face. I suspected that Tara could read the message hiding behind that smile: "Eat my chalk dust, witch."

I watched, holding my breath until I was dizzy, hoping that somehow all the crappy gymnasts had gotten into the end of the line. No such luck. Only two girls out of the twenty-two who had come to tryouts weren't able to make the move on the first or second try.

Marlys Bledsoe, who was in my remedial spells class (and who had just this morning turned a frog into Eminem—

Mr. Phogg had quickly wiped his memory and zapped him back to the oblivion into which he'd fallen), started spinning so fast, the coach had to zap her into one of the padded walls to stop her. I felt for her as she slid down the padded wall. Before her feet hit the floor, she disappeared, her wail of dismay trailing off abruptly.

Despite my fear that the same thing would happen to me, the sight of Marlys sliding down the wall was funny. But I didn't laugh, and neither did the other girls—Marlys had a reputation for turning laughing people into toadstools when she was in the throes of massive humiliation, and we all knew we'd never make the squad if we were toadstools.

Another girl, whose name I hadn't quite caught, would have done fine, except she had this little . . . problem: She disappeared when she cried. And she cried (with joy, I think) when she finished her move successfully. I could relate, because back in fifth grade I'd had a habit of disappearing when I got really upset. Mom had to wipe a lot of memories that year. I waited for Invisi Girl to appear again, so I could offer some sympathy. But apparently she knew she wasn't going to make the cut based on her unfortunate tic, because we all waited for her to reappear to no avail.

After a while, Coach sighed. "Okay, Tara, demonstrate the next one."

Tara sent a nasty little "Try this, scud" smile to me before she raised her arms and rose into the air much faster than last time. She did a series of complicated spins and tucks, ending up on one of the steel beams of the gym, poised like a gymnast on the balance beam. She then dove off, head-first, went into a controlled spin, and pulled out just in time to land on the floor.

Coach Gertie seemed surprised. "My, my. You must think well of these girls, Tara, to give them such a difficult routine."

Tara looked like a picture of innocence. "Was that too difficult?"

"No, no. I'm sure it will help me make my final deci-sions." Coach Gertie glanced at us, lined up waiting like so many puppies in a discount pet shop cage. "It is so difficult. I wish I could take you all."

Behind her, Tara had dropped the innocent act—it prob-ably hurt to keep it up for so long, the beeyotch weeyotch. She looked like she thought we were all going to fail—but she was looking right at me as the first girl stepped up. Great. My first enemy and she's this year's head cheerleader.

I thought I'd been smart, making sure I was at the end of the line. That way, I could scope out the mistakes other girls made and avoid them. Why was it that I kept forget-ting my magic skills were at the remedial level? By the time it was my turn, my stomach was protesting the whole idea of doing a routine in midair. I ignored it. I wanted to make the squad. Strike that. I *needed* to make the squad, and chickening out wasn't going to make it happen.

I raised my arms over my head and shot up faster than I ever had, even in my childhood days, before I'd learned how nervous my magic made Dad. It felt glorious!

I finished the routine and landed on the beam with no problem, even striking a graceful pose (if I do say so myself). It felt good to have something solid under my feet. But then I made the mistake of looking down. Way down. The coach and the other girls looked like they were faraway Munchkins.

You can fly, the practical inner voice in my head said to my lurching and uncertain stomach. *You can fly.* So I told my feet to kiss the beam good-bye, confidently dove off head-first . . . and immediately lost my lunch. I could have sworn I heard Tara chuckle, but it might have been my imagination. Because I was pretty busy trying to figure out which to do first: pull out of the dive or try to hold back the puke.

I would probably have crashed directly into the floor (after showering the girls below me with half-digested curry) if Coach Gertie hadn't acted fast. A bucket at the center of an inverted umbrella appeared below me, protecting those beneath from my unfortunate regurgitation. And just in time. Although I suppose it might have been worth the humiliation to see Tara's perfect uniform messed up.

No such luck. My plunge became a float. The umbrella/ bucket thing disappeared just before it hit the floor, no thanks to me. Coach didn't even look like she was straining to keep me safe as I found myself turning gently in midair and landing on my feet in slow motion. All eyes were on me. So I gave my best Queen Elizabeth wave. I couldn't help it. Happily, everyone laughed. Except Tara. And Coach Gertie.

"It would be best if you went home to recuperate now," Coach said briskly.

"I'm fine." I knew I wasn't. I inherited my mother's fair skin and tendency to turn grayish-blue when I wasn't feeling well, and I could see by the coach's expression that she was afraid I would faint right then and there.

"Nonsense. Go home, Miss Stewart. Tryouts are over."

I was humiliated. I tried to accept defeat, but it was as bitter as the bile in my throat. "I—"

Coach pointed to Tara. "Your head cheerleader and I will discuss the tryouts over the weekend." Coach looked right at me when she added, "I'm proud of all of you for trying your best. If you don't make the team this year, please try again next year."

One of the iffier girls—not as iffy as me, of course—asked timidly, "When will we . . . ?"

Coach smiled the smile of a woman who had heard that question about a zillion times in her lifetime. "The list of those of you who made the team will be posted on the wall Monday afternoon. Have a nice weekend, girls."

A nice weekend? As if. If I were still at Beverly Hills, it would be me and my coach deciding who would work well on the team this year. Instead, I could just imagine the conversation between Coach Gertie and Tara about me. Not that I wanted to go there. But I knew well enough that I would have cut me. I'm a great cheerleader for a mortal school. But put me in the air and I'm a disaster waiting to happen. How could they ignore that?

Maybe it was just time to do a little begging and pleading at home. I'd rather be cheerleading at Beverly Hills High with Chezzie as head cheerleader than stuck in remedial classes at Agatha's without a chance to prove my kewl to the school. As much as I dreaded talking to Mom, it was time for a heart-to-heart. She might just see how important it was for me to go home, where cheerleaders got on the team for groundwork talent—and nobody thought of me as a loser with a capital *L*.

"How did the tryouts go?" Mom was always so cheerfully unaware of how hard it was to be sixteen that I wanted to scream. For the first time I envied mortal kids. They might not be able to fly or summon or cast spells (not that I could do it so well right now either), but at least their parents only had to remember back a few decades to sixteen rather than a few centuries.

"I'm tired. Do you mind?" I had a zillion questions, but

they felt like they were trapped behind a dam. If I let one go, the rest would follow in a rush so loud, the world would go deaf.

My mom never yells. She just raises an eyebrow. It makes it hard to play the beeyotch card. But after my pitiful performance today, I wasn't in the mood to be reasonable, sweet, or even just sulky. I needed to vent. And I could feel myself morphing into super-beeyotch. "Do you think that I want to be interrogated?"

Mom has never been a beeyotch. Ever. At least, not that I've ever seen. Which is sometimes hard to believe, considering Grandmama is listed in the dictionary under the definition. But Mom's always been the oddball in her family (case in point: marrying a mortal and living with almost no magic for nearly twenty years).

Granted, Mom's not as easy on the parental front as my friends have always thought. She likes me to be honest, trustworthy, sensible. I think sensible is the hardest. Sensible meant not using my magic when I was young. Grandmama tells stories about when I was a baby and used to do all sorts of magic. But I don't really remember those times. I just remember Mom's eyebrow raising when I even thought about it. And how Dad's smile would freeze and turn wavy.

"I'm sorry." Mom jumped to—I concede—the most logical conclusion, considering my mood. "I'm sure you'll make it next year."

"Thanks for the vote of confidence," I said as sarcastically as I could. "Actually, we find out Monday." Not that I doubted my all-too-slim chance of being on the list. But I didn't want to tell her that. I wanted to go to my room, pack my bags, and drive my little Jetta to Maddie's, where I could hide in her closet forever with an endless supply of sushi.

"Great!" Mom really sounded as if she didn't have a clue how out of place I was at Agatha's. In Salem. Dad, okay, I could understand why he wouldn't get it. He'd never been a witch. But Mom?

"Don't hold your breath that I'll make the squad. Haven't you heard the news on the witch hotline? The new girl sucks at magic."

"You don't suck at magic. You just need to learn—"

"I've been working hours on my homework. Half of Saturday with Samuel. How long is it going to take me to catch up?" I was trying not to cry, but my voice did come out a little quivery. And then I saw Mom's reaction to my question—a slight hesitation that said it all. "Will I ever?"

"Of course you will, honey. It just takes time." Mom didn't meet my eyes. She just turned away and started scrubbing the kitchen counter. The mortal way, of course. Classic avoidance.

I tried to make the extra sponge scrub another spot farther along the counter. But all it did was hover over the granite countertop like it was waiting for instructions. Great. "Why did you do this to us?"

Mom stopped scrubbing and, with a little wave of her hand, the countertops were clean and the sponges settled themselves on the back of the sink. "It wasn't an easy decision, Prudence, but your father and I agree it was a wise one. Tobias—"

"I'm not talking about Tobias, your gifted-and-*Talented* child. I'm talking about me, the ungifted and Talentless. Why did you raise us as mortals even though we're witches? Did you already know I was going to be a loser?"

"Oh, honey! No! Not at all." Mom started to open the cupboard and take out two glasses, but she stopped and got her "serious talk" look as she sat down at the table. Two glasses of chocolate milk and a plate of peanut butter cookies appeared in front of her. "Magic in the mortal realm can get you into trouble, especially when you're young. And"— she bit her lip as she confessed—"it upset your father, since he can't do magic."

I wasn't interested in milk and cookies, even if they did smell very peanut buttery. "Then why couldn't we just have stayed in Beverly Hills? I have zero chance of making the squad, Mom. And if that's not bad enough, I'm never going to get out of remedial spells!"

"I know it's hard for you right now. And I'm sorry. I thought we could live just fine without magic. But when

Tobias started having trouble controlling his powers, I realized I was wrong." Mom looked like she might come over to hug me, but one look at my face told her the welcome mat was *not* rolled out. "But I promise, you are not a loser when it comes to witchcraft. You'll learn."

"Will I? I am half mortal, after all."

"Of course you will. A witch is a witch is a witch. If you were going to be mortal, you wouldn't be able to summon a paper plate, never mind levitate!"

"Really?" I wasn't sure I believed her. There was something about the way she said it that made it sound like she was leaving out something important. "So why haven't I manifested a Talent yet?"

"I'm sure that since you're now practicing magic instead of avoiding it, you'll manifest a Talent in no time at all."

I still didn't buy it. But I have seen the value of hard work. Or, at least I had back in Beverly Hills. "So you're saying all I have to do is cram sixteen years of magic practice into the next few weeks and my Talent will manifest?" I summoned one of the cookies and took a small bite. Yum.

At that, Mom looked more nervous than she should have. "I wouldn't go that far, honey. There's no need to rush things."

No need to *rush* things? Right. The tiny bite of cookie felt like a stone going down as I swallowed. It was time for Mom to understand that I may have been slotted into remedial magic classes, but I was still no slouch when it came to understanding the way the world worked. "Right now I'm studying like crazy and *barely* managing to maintain my grades."

"You'll catch up. You're doing so well."

Sigh. Why is it that parents think if they say something often enough, you'll believe it? "Mom! I just came back from a cheerleading tryout session that made me wonder if I'll *ever* cut it in the witchworld. And Chezzie was named head cheerleader, so even if we go back to Beverly Hills, I'll have to spend the year watching her take the credit. My choices are very simple: Get up to speed at Agatha's in record time, or go home."

"Going home for us, right now, is not—"

I didn't want to hear any more reasons. I'd heard them all before. I felt my hair lift around my head as I tried to keep my anger in. "I know you guys can't go, because of Tobias. I get it. I don't want to unleash another Chernobyl on the world because that pipsqueak didn't get trained properly."

I took a deep breath. I was trying to hold it in, I really was. But my cookie spun out of my hand, smacking into the cabinets, leaving smears and crumbles everywhere until there was no cookie left. Whoa. I hadn't had a temper tantrum like that since I was little. It was time for a little yoga breathing. I closed my eyes so I wouldn't see Mom staring at the peanut butter cookie decorated kitchen. I breathed in. I breathed out. My hair stopped writhing around my head.

"I know you guys are stuck here." I worked very hard to keep my voice calm, with no wobbling. "But *I* can go home. Maddie's mom will let me stay with her. There's no reason my life needs to be ruined because Tobias is a gifted-and-Talented warlock who needs some serious controls." I opened my eyes. No more peanut butter cookie mess. Apparently, Mom had taken advantage of my breathing to zap the kitchen clean.

Mom wanted to just say no. I could see it in her eyes. But, instead, she said, "First, let's try some heavy-duty tutoring."

"By you? Because Samuel is great, you know. He's taught me a lot. But he's just a kid, like me."

Mom sighed. "I think your learning witchcraft is similar to your learning to drive."

"You mean—"

"We hired a driving tutor for you. It's time for a spells tutor. And maybe a potions tutor, too," Mom said as she waved away the rest of the cookies and the milk.

I thought of Mr. Bindlebrot. "There's this teacher—"

"Never mind. I have the perfect tutor in mind. He's my cousin and he's helped young witches learn the proper casting and stirring methods for four hundred years."

Four hundred years? Great. An old guy. I hoped he

didn't drool when he talked. "When do I start?"

"As soon as I track him down." Mom opened a kitchen drawer and took out salt and her divining crystal.

After ten minutes, in which she tried various locating spells, Mom bit her lip. "Well, it may take a little while. He's a bit of a free spirit. But I'll get him, I promise."

I was feeling better. I guess Mom could tell, because she finally came across the room and hugged me. For a minute I felt like I was six again. All safe and warm and loved. But then I remembered the awful truth. And I knew what I had to do. "Mom?" I still had my head buried in her shoulder. "Will you promise that if this tutor thing doesn't work out, you'll let me go live with Maddie?"

"If you like." I knew there was a catch to her agreement, I could hear it in her voice. Mom never ran from the truth, although sometimes she did this flirty little dance around it. Usually, that made me want to scream. Other times, it made me glad she was my mom. Like now. I guess I just needed to believe there was a soft place for me to fall if I really was the Loser of Witchville and Mom was too afraid to tell me so.

Chapter 12

MADDIE: A car?!

ME: Yep

MADDIE: Didnt think ur dad would ever

ME: Me either

MADDIE: Any boys 2 go drivin with? Better
yet parking?

ME: Sorry 1950! Since when does grounded
girl know about parking?

Maddie's texts was so lighthearted that I couldn't bring myself to discuss my own sticky predicament. Besides, exactly how would I explain that I had to cram a lifetime's worth of magic into a few months? So I decided just to err on the side of letting her babble along happily. Not that that didn't cause me a little pang of homesickness.

Maddie's parents had been as strict as mine, so her comment about parking really shocked me. But I suppose it was only natural. Now that her dad was off to his new life and her mom was on her own and dating, Maddie had the Grand Parent Canyon to fall into. You know, that place where both parents are under the impression the kid is safe between them, but there's just empty space because the kid is off having fun.

Or getting into trouble. I didn't know whether to be worried about Maddie's freedom by distraction, or wish I could be there to share it.

Still. Maddie had always been sensible, even in the rare moments when her parents weren't watching. I would just have to hope she didn't lead on the wrong guy. Guy handling was a tricky business. Even I was having trouble with it, as I discovered that evening at my tutoring session with Samuel.

"I hear you tried to share my curry with all the other cheerleaders."

Samuel was definitely getting too familiar—both with my mom's cooking and with me. But since Mom hadn't yet located this great cousin/tutor she had promised me, I didn't mention his overstep. But I didn't smile or encourage him either.

He got the message, I guess, because he pulled out a

wand and my spell book and said, "You said you wanted to learn how to handle more magic at once?"

"Right." I gave him my best perky can-do smile. "I just want to learn everything I didn't learn about magic in Beverly Hills this weekend." I'd had to confess to him that while I could levitate, I had not been able to master casting even a simple spell like the confetti toss at the same time. Humiliating, I know. But I wasn't going to get better if I didn't know where I needed to push.

"You're ambitious, aren't you?" He seemed to find that funny. He handed me the wand and explained that I should use it to focus my spells as I held myself just a few inches off the ground.

I didn't listen, of course. I wanted to go fast. So I levitated to the ceiling, pointed my wand, started with "Sparkle, glitter, gleam . . . ," and promptly fell to the floor in a heap. Oh yeah, I'm a natural.

I practiced until I could levitate, somersault twice, and summon a top hat and a rabbit at the same time (summoning while levitating is just a bit easier than casting a spell, for me at least). I was black-and-blue by the time Samuel was satisfied that I could handle everything smoothly and simultaneously. I was also exhausted, but still determined to master both simultaneous magic and midair spinning.

I held my position near the ceiling and carefully summoned my cell phone to Samuel's hand. "Here, snap me in action."

He looked at the phone in confusion. "This is a camera?"

I came down from my levitation carefully and showed him how to snap my picture, then got back into position. "Now! Take two in case one doesn't come out."

He did, and then, being Samuel, he started examining the phone, flipping up the various lenses of his glasses every now and then.

"Why do you have a camera on the phone?" He never hesitated to ask me questions. Which was annoying. He never seemed to be suspicious, though, just curious. Which was endearing.

"It was a guilty conscience gift from my folks, to make up for being ripped from my home. With it, I can stay in touch with my friends back in Beverly Hills," I explained.

"Is it some mortal thing? Taking pictures while you talk on the phone?"

His habit of assuming everything was some mortal secret was not so endearing. "Tedious" comes to mind as a good adjective. Which really brings out the beeyotch in me.

"Yep. The picture captures the soul, and then the mortals can take it home and burn it."

Apparently the idea wasn't that absurd, because he didn't seem to get that I was kidding. "Does that destroy the other person's soul?" He actually held the phone a little farther away from him while he asked. Dope.

"Nope. Just makes the person whose picture got burned

have to be the slave of the one who burned it."

"Neat."

Another annoying trait of Samuel's is that he likes to use archaic mortal phrases. I suspect he watches lots of mortal TV when he isn't in school teaching Maria and Denise how to be the ultimate geekoids—or over at my house studying my dad as if he's a science experiment.

Not that I would ask Samuel about what he liked to do in his spare time. Questions like that seem innocent, but they can cause big problems. You don't want to make a guy think you're more interested in him than you are. It can only lead to drama and lots of useless talking.

Of course, it's not like I know this firsthand. I haven't had a serious boyfriend yet. My dad won't let me.

I know. There are ways around protective dads. But not magical moms. I've probably mentioned that if I'm alone with a boy for more than sixty seconds, I break out in big weepy hives. Attractive. You could consider me a babe magnet. Or is that maggot?

Which made me realize: I'd been alone with Mr. Bindlebrot for more than sixty seconds. Not much. But no hives. Maybe the spell only worked on mortal boys?

It was worth checking out. Even retro games of spin the bottle are no fun when you're spell-binded. Quick kisses are fun, but I wouldn't mind knowing what it felt like to have a boy's lips on mine for longer than forty-five seconds. Not that you can't get a great kiss out of such a short time. I think the boys almost liked that I played hard-to-kiss.

I'd have to figure out a way to investigate the mortal/witch thing. A few weeks in magic class—remedial or not—had taught me that one word in a spell can make a huge difference to the result.

Only one way to find out. But not, thank you very much, with a guy who believes cell phone cameras can steal souls.

"Why would a mortal want to destroy anyone's soul?" Sometimes Samuel is so earnest, I can't bear to laugh.

I sighed. "I was just kidding. The camera just makes communication feel so much closer. I can talk to my friend in L.A. and show her a picture of my room." Not that I had.

"Oh." He blushed. "I'm a little geeky about mortal stuff. Sorry."

Duh! "Don't worry about it. I have relatives who are much worse, believe me. Thanks for tutoring me. I owe you a good lunch tomorrow."

"It's fun to help you. Your dad is neat. And your mom is great. I've never met a witch like her." He didn't bring up the camera thing again, so neither did I.

Yes. Samuel did have a crush thing going for me—maybe even for my dad the mortal and my mom the unconventional witch. And no, I wasn't going to break his heart yet. I was already bottom of the heap after my performance at tryouts, and I needed him desperately.

"See you tomorrow?" Samuel looked like a hopeful puppy dog.

"I guess." I didn't want to seem too eager. From the angst about breakups and makeups I'd heard in the hallway at Agatha's, I was sure the boy-girl thing translated well from mortal to witchworld. And in either world, a girl didn't want to give any boy the idea he was indispensable. That's when he'd start to make demands.

Samuel inexplicably turned and smiled at the wall near the TV. "You should join us next time, squirt."

"Who are you talking to?" There wasn't a ghost there. At least, not one that I could see. The ghosts had better things to do than watch me make a black-and-blue fool out of myself.

Samuel just kept talking to the wall. "I can show you how to disappear so your outline doesn't shimmer."

I couldn't help squealing in outrage when I saw the shimmering outline I'd mistaken for a convoluted sunbeam solidify into my brother. "Mom!"

"Okay, okay." Dorklock held up his hands in surrender. "I'm leaving. What do you care? It wasn't like you were kissing him or anything."

Samuel turned the same orange hue as his favorite spice. But when Dorklock turned to ask him, with the shining young face that adults couldn't seem to resist, "Do you mean it? About the outline," he nodded.

"Cool!" Dorklock levitated, spun as gracefully as a dork can, and filled the air above his spinning body with confetti. At the same time. Effortlessly.

"Get out, or . . ."

He was gone, leaving behind the lingering aroma of twelve-year-old boy and a snowstorm of confetti on the floor.

I'd thought I wrecked things with Daniel when I ran away without saying a word after he invited me to play hooky. But the next morning at my locker, I discovered I'd written him off too early.

I heard the whispers start before I even saw Daniel beside me. "So, Cinderella 666. Why did you do the pumpkin act on me? You could have just said no. Even better, you could have said yes. We'd have had some fun."

I shrugged. "Sorry." Everyone was watching us again, and I longed for the days when I was a known quantity, not the new girl-half-breed raised in the mortal world with the haunted locker number 666. I needed to start bringing my reputation in line right away.

"Don't you ever get tired of being a good girl?" He was looking right into my eyes, and he had this grin that was so bad-boy that at least a dozen actors would have demanded their plastic surgeons duplicate it, if they'd seen it.

"Not enough to risk detention." I didn't even like the spa

mud wraps all my friends at home went ga-ga for, so an hour in quicksand seemed like a really bad idea to me. Although it was tempting to try to step into the bad-girl role that Daniel, the quintessential bad boy, had offered me, I had a feeling I wouldn't ever be too good at it. After all, if I'd been good at being bad, wouldn't I have ignored my parents when they said not to use magic like my brother? And wouldn't I know enough magic not to be stuck in a remedial class? Besides, I was going to try to talk myself into a pity place on the team if I hadn't made the list. Playing hooky could mess that up big-time.

"I'd make sure you didn't get caught. No one would ever know the 666 Girl had eighty-sixed it out of here for a little while."

I laughed, and—I must have been light-headed because his face was so close to mine—made a confession I never should have made. "My mom has a spell on me. If I'm near a boy for more than a minute alone, I break out in these really gross, weepy hives."

He pulled back a little, and for a minute I was afraid I'd broken out as I spoke to him. "She does?"

"My mom's a bit overprotective." I felt defensive, and surprised at the way he'd gone from hot to cold—even though that was what I wanted. Well, maybe hot to still warm was what I'd been aiming for.

"And you let that stop you?" he asked scornfully.

"What?"

"I had assumed you were like me—not meant for remedial class, but I guess if you haven't figured out how to counter that lame spell . . ."

He popped out, leaving me alone to ponder the fact that I was no longer his Cinderella Girl, but was instead back to being the 666 Girl—with big weepy hives for decoration.

He'd also left me wondering if I'd ever get the chance to ask him to help me find a way around my mom's protective spells in the same way I found a way around her mortal rules about swearing (it doesn't count if you stretch it out . . . so beeyotch, sheeyoot, daminee cricket) and being out past curfew. I already knew what I could offer him: a ride in my Jetta. Parking optional, but very much on the table.

Chapter 13

MADDIE: Danny Trimball asked me out!!!

ME: DT? Brace Face? Did U puke?

MADDIE: I forgot U haven't seen him Hold
4 pix

ME: Losin the braces makes a big diff!

MADDIE: N spendin the summer on his
grandfatherz horse farm made him a hottie

ME: A hottie? Hez no hottie. Hez a torcher! Id
hop a broom right now if he wasnt already
taken

MADDIE: Maybe Samuel has a grandfather
with a horse farm

ME: Samuel would need a trip 2 the best

plastic surgeon in 90210 And some heavy
duty protein drinks 2

MADDIE: Harsh He dance?

ME: Dunno Don't wanna kno. Hez good 4
whats inside his skull not whats outside

MADDIE: U tellin me theres no hotties at ur
new HS? Noway U need glasses

ME: What do U want from me? Pix

MADDIE: Good idea Film at 11

ME: Noway

MADDIE: Uve got that cute lil camera Use it
Snap some of the runner ups Maybe Uve
overlooked some1

ME: Noway

MADDIE: Way

ME: K But Ive got 2 practice my moves 1st
Made the team!

I decided to humor Maddie as much as I could. She was
still my best friend, even if she was all the way across the
continent. After all, she wouldn't be able to tell I was in a
school of witches just by looking at them—as long as I was
careful to keep the rabbits, spell books, and flying erasers
out of the shot. So I took the camera to school. Why not?
After all, I made the cheerleading squad. Yep. I did. Miracles
do happen in real life, just like on TV.

Well, semi-miracles, anyway. My name wasn't on the list of those who had made the team. But I got a note from Coach Gertie to come and see her. I didn't want to, but too bad. It was my last chance to convince her I would learn what I needed to know at lightspeed.

So I showed up at practice and tried not to hate the girls who were celebrating having made the team. I didn't know how to begin to beg. After all, I couldn't look needy. I had to beg with confidence. Unfortunately, after my dismal performance and my definitely un-stellar tutoring session with Samuel, I had a confidence level of zip.

"How are you feeling?" Coach smiled at me, but I could tell she was looking me over for signs of weakness.

"I'm great. No problems at all. In fact, I was practicing all weekend—"

"Great!" Coach cut me off. "I need you well enough to begin practice next week."

All the confident begging I'd hoped to do rushed out of my head at once. I had only one thought. One question. "I made the team?" I couldn't keep the incredulity out of my voice—and I was not deaf to the murmur of wonder that did the wave through the other girls.

Tara couldn't be ignored, though. "Coach! She can't even do a simple midair vault and dismount. She'll kill someone if you let her on the team."

Coach looked at me, and I could see her actually weighing Tara's words. Kill someone? Myself, maybe, but unless I fell directly on someone too slow to get out of the way, that was a bit harsh. I protested, in fine cheerleader fashion. "I'll do extra practice until I get the move right, Coach."

"Good attitude. Others could learn from you. After all, you *have* been on a championship team."

"A mortal team, Coach!" Tara protested.

"True." Coach looked at me, then nodded, a swift no-nonsense jerk of her chin. "Still. If we decided to enter the championships, we'd have to follow the mortal rules. Prudence will be on probation until she learns our magic routines. Mortal games only."

Probation? Me? Crappaccino. I hated the word. The concept. The reality, even. But I did what any good cheerleader would do: I smiled on the outside and blazed like a Christmas tree doused with gasoline on the inside.

Coach smiled, a real smile that was nothing more than her satisfaction with her call and her blind adult belief that I was happy with her decision. "I like your spirit, girl. Can't hardly be blamed for not being able to do what you've not been taught. But you'll get it. I can tell." She frowned, as if she might have been too positive. "If you work hard."

"I love to work hard," I assured her with a surprisingly steady voice. The Christmas tree inferno and the weekend of despair and practice with Samuel had taken a lot out of me.

"Good. Then today why don't you work hard on learning to keep your lunch where it belongs when you spin."

"Yes, ma'am."

I'm no dummy. I've been cheerleading since sixth grade. I'd gotten the sympathy admit—or maybe the novelty admit, since it fascinated Coach Gertie that I had gone to a mortal school for twelve years (including kindergarten, which my teachers and fellow students alike seemed to find a ridiculous concept. Apparently a roomful of four- and five-year-old witches could make a five hundred-year-old warlock's hair turn permanently and irrevocably gray). I had a lot to prove.

Still, I was on the team, probation or not. That felt good. So maybe I couldn't tell Maddie all about my woes, but I could make her happy with a few pics.

First, of course, I popped into the boys' locker room for a few candids of Mr. Bindlebrot. Just kidding! I thought about it. Hard. But if anyone saw a picture of Mr. Bindlebrot in a towel, I don't think even my mother's magic could keep me in the school. Some things just cross a line in any world. Besides, I didn't want to share that view with anyone, not even my best friend. Not even if she lived on the other side of the country and didn't have popping powers. Sure, Bindlebrot was only a crush, but he was my crush and I didn't want to share.

There weren't many candidates for hottie, but I knew

Maddie wouldn't believe me unless I showed her. So I stationed myself in the hallway by my locker (I took a picture of it, too, knowing she'd get a kick out of locker 666 even though I couldn't tell her about Hi, the resident ghost).

I snapped the tall boy who was new, like me. He'd found a way to fit it (tall equals basketball, even in witchworld).

I caught Daniel, in profile, so she wouldn't see exactly how cute he was—or she'd text-tease me mercilessly. He didn't look my way, but it was too soon to tell if it was because he was over me or trying to get me to change my mind about jumping the school fence (metaphorically speaking) with him.

The boy three lockers down from me had promise, if he washed and brushed his hair and got rid of the unibrow he had going. We didn't share any classes, but being practically locker buddies meant that was not an obstacle to a drive-by eye lock. I knew girls back in L.A. who were experts at the art.

I went to lunch full of my good deeds, knowing that I'd made Maddie happy and proved my point that there weren't many candidates for hottie in my new school. No doubt she'd share that info with the other cheerleaders, and Chezzie would be pleased.

At lunch, I had a decision to make. Should I eat with Samuel, Maria, and Denise, the fringies who had been there for me on the first awful days of school? Or the cheerleaders, who weren't going to be there for me until they'd made sure I was one of them? Probation made things tricky. But the longer I stayed at a fringie table, the harder the move would be.

I know the choice should have been clear, but really, all I wanted was to sit down with my friends, fringies or not, and just talk. But that wasn't the way to bond with the squad. I'd told the lunch trio what I intended to do this morning in the hallway before our first class. They were looking at me with big smiles of encouragement. So why did that make it even harder? Sigh.

When I walked up to the cheerleaders' table, I could sense that disaster was about to strike. They tensed and shrank together in more unison than they showed on the floor. Not a good sign. I flipped past the thought that I should just keep on walking over to sit with Samuel, Maria, and Denise. I understand the high school jungle, even with the witch twist. It was now or never.

I set my tray down in midair, where it hovered perfectly, despite my quivering nerves. Taking out the cell phone, I pointed it toward the group. "Smile!"

"What's that?" Tara asked, her lip curling as if I'd pulled out a dead toad.

"It's a mortal toy called a cell phone, and it takes pictures." I pantomimed taking a picture and said as brightly as I could, "Say cheese, everyone!"

My instinct had been correct: Witch cheerleaders are as

vain as mortal cheerleaders. They twitched their hair and makeup to perfection with practiced finger flutters, then smiled. Big, bright cheerleader smiles.

I handed the camera to a smirking boy and quickly joined the group for the picture. Everyone oohed when I got the camera back and showed them the square at the back where they could see it. We looked good. My smile was just as bright as anyone else's. No one looking at the picture would have had a clue that I was the new witch on the block—and on probation, at that. So I promised to make copies for the entire squad.

I thought I was master of my domain until later that night, when Samuel came for dinner and another session of tutoring.

"Missed you at lunch today. But we were all glad you're on the team now, since you wanted it so much."

"Thanks. I missed you guys too." Which, surprisingly, was true. It was really too bad that fringies and being kewl didn't mix well at school. Not that I planned to snub Samuel, Maria, or Denise. Ever.

But, even though lunch wasn't a problem for Samuel, apparently something else was. "Why didn't you take my picture? You took everyone else's." He wasn't exactly subtle, and he was way too observant.

I hadn't meant to hurt his feelings. "I was just trying to capture the atmosphere around the lockers for Maddie." I'd told him a lot about my life back in Beverly Hills, and about Maddie, during our tutoring sessions.

"Oh." Oddly enough for a mortal groupie, he didn't believe me. I could tell by the way he shrank away from me just a little.

"No. Really, Samuel. She doesn't know I go to a witch school." I decided to come clean, sort of. "She wants to know if there are any hot guys in the school, and I'm trying to prove to her there aren't—so I didn't take your picture."

"You think I'm hot?" Again, he wasn't buying it.

I thought about lying, but it was just too cruel. And, besides, it could cause complications I didn't want to deal with. But first, I had to be sure we were not being spied on. "Before I answer a question like that, I need a quick sweep of the room—any invisible Dorklocks around?"

He didn't smile, but he did check carefully, flipping his lenses as he scanned the room. "No one but us. Camera Girl and No-Photo Boy."

"Okay. It's dangerous to ask if you're hot, you know?"

He shrugged. "I can take it."

"Well." I pretended to consider him carefully, from the scraggly part in his straight brown hair to the scuffed toes of his dark brown boots. "Definitely warm—if you took off those glasses."

He smiled. "I never take off my glasses." I could see that my not labeling him a hottie had made him believe me. Good call on my part.

"Why is that, by the way?" I hoped I wouldn't offend him, but I was really burning to know why such a smart kid with otherwise vanilla fashion sense would wear a pair of glasses that had three separate lenses—red, blue, and green—with little levers to raise and lower them. They were kind of like the glasses that Benjamin Franklin made in the movie *National Treasure*.

"They help me see the other dimensions more easily," Samuel explained.

"Other dimensions?" For a minute I thought he was losing it big-time.

But, no, he was just into that science thing. "They're quantum glasses, based on string theory in physics. With them, I can see the other dimensions that are nearby."

"Sure." I wasn't going to get into it. Not a chance. I like science, but biology is way more interesting than physics. Atoms and quarks and things you can see with the naked eye are just not the same thing as the way the brain works. I had decided back in mortal school that I'd be a doctor. A pediatrician, to be exact. I didn't need to see into other dimensions. I just needed a warm stethoscope. And lollipops.

"Want to try them?" I guess my silence had seemed like skepticism rather than disinterest.

I shrugged. "Sure. Why not."

He took them off and handed them over, giving me a

glimpse of very nice brown eyes. Just to add authenticity to my excuse for not snapping him, I lifted the phone and snapped him. "There. Too bad for me. Maddie's just going to see one more cutie in the school. You shouldn't hide your eyes." Not that I thought he'd take my fashion advice.

The compliment had a curious effect. Besides blushing bright red, his eyes turned gold near the irises. Interesting.

I put on the glasses and immediately felt dizzy. Lights, colors, even sounds seemed to come at me as if I were in a tunnel with a dozen trains rushing toward me. I took them off and gave Samuel a shaky smile. "Great. Where'd you get these? Maybe I'll pick up a pair for the Dorklock."

"My mom and I made them . . . before she died. They're the only pair in the world."

My already high respect for his abilities went up a notch. But I tried not to show him that. "I guess you letting me use your glasses means I have to let you ride in my car." I paused a beat for his response and was not disappointed.

"A car?" Samuel didn't even put his glasses back on, he was so interested.

"A yellow Jetta." Dad may have downsized the car, but I wasn't letting him change the color.

"You'd really let me ride in it?" he asked eagerly.

Great. Samuel had given me the answer I was looking for:

a car was cool, even in the witch world. Better, the mention of the car had completely driven away his insecurity that I hadn't taken his picture. Am I good or am I good? Disaster averted once more. I was starting to get the hang of the witchworld. At least, so I thought until I got to cheerleading practice five minutes late the next day.

Tara, as head cheerleader, had the right to call me to order. But, in my opinion, she didn't have the right to enjoy it so much.

"Hey! Prudence. You're late," she sneered.

"I had to talk to Mr. Phogg."

"The remedial teacher? Are you failing?" She glommed on to that pretty quickly. I guess she was hoping I'd say yes and she could legitimately get me off the team.

"No. I just wanted to arrange moving up to regular magic classes," I replied patiently.

Which was true. And it was a pleasure to see her frustration that she still had me on her squad—and at her lunch table. That I had been late because of a desperate, and unsuccessful, attempt to convince Phogg to move me up was another story. One that I wasn't going to tell her. Especially after she made me do a hundred pushups as punishment for tardiness. The weeyotch.

I did tell Maddie, though.

ME: This teacher hates me

MADDIE: Not U Ur the student with the mostest

ME: Right But he doesnt even give me
brownie points 4 out of class tutorin

MADDIE: Wassup?

ME: I think its cause Im diff He doesnt think
Im good enuf

MADDIE: Diff? How?

ME: Probably cause Im from Cali Hez not
fond of newbies

Right. Sometimes it was a pain trying to explain things to Maddie while keeping a healthy distance from the truth: I'm half mortal, and my teacher is seriously old school. Like Plato and Socrates old school. Which had never been clearer than when I tried to ask him—practically begged him—to kick me upstairs.

"You're making excellent progress in my class, Miss Stewart," he said. Which was a promising beginning.

"Thank you, sir. Do you think I'm ready for the regular class?" I tried not to look too desperate for a yes, but I suspect I failed, because he recoiled a bit.

"Let's not get ahead of ourselves."

"But I've mastered summoning—I can do twenty things at once. With control."

"Summoning isn't everything, Miss Stewart."

He'd been saying this to me all month. Despite the fact I'd been adding magic tricks to my repertoire at the rate of two per night. Some teachers just label you and you can never escape their label. Apparently, I was labeled remedial, and remedial I would stay if it was up to this teacher.

Which it wasn't. My mom could eat him alive—or at least summon a lion to eat him alive. But I didn't want to drag Mom into this. I just wanted to get out of the remedial classes. I had no doubt that the regular spells class would be tougher to pass, but I was tired of learning the same thing over and over. I needed to learn faster than molasses in wintertime.

"What can I do to prove to you I'm ready for regular spell class?" I asked.

He seemed surprised. His mouth opened and closed like a fish's. "It's usual to finish out the year and then take your placement test for next year—"

"I don't want to wait until next year!" I wailed, feeling like a two-year-old. But I knew it was the one thing Skin and Bones hated worse than passing someone out of remedial spells when the school year had barely begun.

With a desperate little gasp, he said, "Fine, fine. If you want to prove you're ready for regular spell class, you'll have to—" I could see his glassy little eyes spinning as he thought. "You'll have to summon a thousand objects at once, turn your classmates into toads and back again without letting them know, and build the Empire State Building with LEGOs without touching a piece with your hands." He sat back, rubbing his eyes as if they were tired from all that spinning, and then fixed the beady things back on me with a smile. "By the end of December."

"By—" I protested, knowing instinctively that what he was asking was unfair.

"Otherwise, you'll be in remedial all year, Miss Stewart." The little toad thought he'd won. For a long moment, I fought the urge to turn him into the toad he was. But that was baby stuff. And I wasn't a baby. I was a high school junior who didn't want to be in remedial spells any longer than necessary.

I stood up and smiled brilliantly, just to confuse him. "December? Excellent. You won't mind if I aim to make that before Christmas, do you? I enjoy the holidays so much more when I don't have a test weighing on my mind."

Which is when I popped out of his classroom, five minutes late to practice and right into the slavering jaws of Tara the Terrible. Life is so unfair.

Chapter 14

MADDIE: Whats with the fashion faux pas?
Who is that guy?
ME: The kids at Agathas have a really umm
unique sense of style
MADDIE: Fur? I can appreciate a good mink
But that dude looks like he clubbed his
clothes
ME: LOL U should see what he eats 4 lunch
MADDIE: Still Maybe U should show ur mom
ur pix That might send her home fast
ME: As if When my mom commits shez rabid
MADDIE: LOL! Gtg Where are the rest of
those pix?

ME: Incoming

MADDIE: Kewl Wish me luck on my basket

toss Ive finally lost enough 2 B a flyer

ME: Fly high anorexic chick! N send pix!

Maddie's not really anorexic. She's just wanted to be a flyer since fifth grade. But she'd never quite been able to ditch the ice cream and cookies that kept her fifteen pounds too padded for the job of being lifted into the air.

Now she had finally lost the weight. And I wasn't there to see her fly. Or to make sure the other cheerleaders were there to catch her when she fell. Or even to see her go out on a date with the now acceptably cute Danny Trimball. I couldn't even get her to come along on my first ride in the car. Or on the first babysitting job to pay for said car.

Babysitting is not what it's cracked up to be. I'd agreed to watch our (mortal) neighbor's baby because (besides needing the forty dollars they promised me) I figured that a kid who couldn't even turn over in her crib would give me lots of time to practice my spells homework.

Wrong! The baby cried from the moment she woke up (five minutes after her parents left with big smiles and a long list of numbers where they could be reached) until five minutes before they came home, just shy of midnight. Baby radar.

Despite disastrous baby caper #1, I was pleased to deposit the check into my car fund, as well as act delighted that they wanted to make this a weekly deal. But I did decide to check out the spell book for a "soothe the baby" spell for any and all future babysitting expeditions.

There was a whole section, it seemed. At last I understood how Mom had always gotten the Dorklock to stay in the corner during time-out. This spell was written in her own hand, which meant that she'd created it—out of desperation, no doubt.

I wondered if I'd ever see my own handwritten spells here. Somehow, the family spell book had made my being a witch more real than the fact that I could summon objects or fly. There were spells in a spidery handwriting so old that Grandmama said it was from her own grandmother. Mind-boggling. I couldn't even read them, because they were written in Old English. Grandmama said it was a translation from something older. Sanskrit, maybe. She wasn't sure. Those family scrolls had been lost in the years after the translation was done.

Generations and millennia of witches had added to the spell book. But if I couldn't learn what I needed to know, and manifest a Talent, I would not be one of them. Skin and Bones didn't want to let me go, and at the rate he taught magic, I wouldn't ever learn what I needed to know to cheerlead in a real magic game. Or pass the Wisdom Test.

Even Dorklock was better at simple spells than I was. Hecate, he was better at complex spells too. Mom had recently discovered that he'd been popping himself home for visits with his friends. He'd been grounded in every way—magic and mortal—my parents could think of. Poor Dad had turned gray when he realized that Tobias could sneak around Mom like that already.

I could just see it now: Samuel, like his mother before him, being the youngest to pass the test, with the Dorklock right behind him. And me, raised by mortals, being the oldest.

As if I wasn't facing a life of living in the magic slow lane, I was blowing it in math, too. I never had trouble in math. Until I started trying to stuff eleven years of magic instruction into a month.

I had noticed that Mr. Bindlebrot no longer automatically approved my equations—sending the glowing letters fading into the air. Several times, in fact, he had stood there clearing his throat while I noticed an error and fixed it.

This time, he didn't give me a chance to notice. He smiled his great Bloom-quality smile, bringing back memories of the towel and drops of water on bare skin. And then he said, very kindly, "Your math is slipping." My respectably glowing equation did not disappear. Instead, it pulsed red.

"Oh, criminey. I forgot to square *x*."

I fixed the equation quickly, but it didn't disappear as Mr. Bindlebrot stood there, staring at me. "Do you need some extra help, Prudence?"

"No." I denied, and then kicked myself. "Maybe." I realized I had a primo excuse to try out a scientific hypothesis of mine—whether I could be alone with a male witch for more than sixty seconds without breaking into hives. "I've just been so busy. Perhaps I could speak to you after school?"

My equation finally disappeared.

He seemed puzzled, but he agreed. "Certainly."

I didn't hear a word he said for the rest of the class. Although I did make note of the homework assignment when he gave it. It helped that he summoned a gong and rang it to get our attention right before he gave homework. I wish all my teachers did that.

True to his word, after my last class disappeared, instead of being popped to the hallway, I found it was, at last, just me and Mr. Bindlebrot (sadly, I don't think that would make a good song lyric). "How can I help you get back on track, Prudence? Would you like to arrange some after-school tutoring sessions?"

Right. Not even if he promised to wear the towel! After school I had practice—and I needed every minute of it to convince Coach I should come off probation status. "I'm just a little tired. If you could assign me some makeup work, I know I could—"

"Do you realize you have dropped from an A to an F on your daily quiz?"

"An F?" Umm, no. If I'd realized that, I'd have done my math homework instead of going online to find the answers. Blastini! I didn't need my math aptitude to go belly up on me now.

I had schemed all class on how to keep the conversation going for at least two minutes. But it didn't look like it would be hard now. We were seventy-five seconds in, no sign of hives, and my grade was on the line. The only thing worse would be for the hives to pop out right now.

They didn't. However, ninety seconds into this rather abysmal experiment, my mother did.

Mr. Bindlebrot didn't seem too surprised. "Good to see you again. Prudence and I were just discussing her math." His natural magnetism didn't have the same impact as when he was only wearing a towel, but I did see Mom blink before she smiled back.

Good to see you again? When had they met before? Had Mom been checking up on my grades?

"How wonderful to see you after so long." She glanced around the classroom, where equations were glowing in the air all around us. "You've done well."

He shrugged. "Teaching at Agatha's is a challenge, but I

always liked challenges, as I'm sure you remember."

Was he flirting? With my mother? I wanted to die.

He turned to smile at me, but the wattage was dimming and the jolt failed to reach my heart. "Did your mother tell you that she was my first girlfriend?"

Yuck. Another crush bites the dust.

"Don't you have to make practice, honey?" Mom smiled at me, and I knew that she intended to stay there, talking about me with Mr. Bindlebrot. Which would have been okay, now that my crush had dried up and blown away like powdered makeup in a desert wind. Except that it meant she was going to find out about my slipping math grades way before report card time. Bummer.

Things actually looked up at practice, though. Not that my skills were hugely improved. But I found out what it was Coach was thinking when she let me stay on the team. "I hoped you might show us some of the routines you learned at your mortal school." She was oh so casual (so she thought) as she added, "The ones that won you the championship, perhaps."

"Sure." I had created quite a few routines. It was something I was good at. In the mortal world. "The routines I know don't use magic." Well, none that I would admit to—if it got back to Mom, there'd be a talking-to.

"That's fine. We couldn't use magic in competition, either, because all the competitions are with mortals."

Tara was not happy. "But our next game is a–"

"I'm not thinking of our next game." Coach had a weird glint in her eyes. "I'm thinking of the regional competition."

There was a gasp and a moment of silence.

Tara dropped her smile in favor of total confusion expressed by downturned lips and a big old frown line down the center of her forehead. A first. I wished I had my cell phone. The snap would be priceless. "Regional competition? But, we never–"

"This year, we will. After all, we have a secret weapon: Prudence was going to be head cheerleader at a mortal high school that won the national tournament last year. She obviously knows how to win."

Clearly Coach Gertie had been checking out the rep of my old school. Apparently, even witches had learned to like the Internet for research. I shrugged, trying to give the impression that I didn't know what a bombshell my first suggestion was going to be. "First thing you have to do is stop spending all your time practicing magic routines."

Tara took it as well as could be expected. After a split-second gape, she whispered, "Are you out of your mind?"

Sometimes. "Your technique is sloppy. And if you're going to be sloppy, you might get a pity clap at Regionals, but you'll never make it to Nationals." I knew it was a bomb, but I don't think anyone in the gym could tell I did. I am a consummate cheerleader, after all: attitude over reality.

"Out of the question!" Tara wasn't happy. Although, to give her her props, it was only obvious to another cheerleader.

"We can spare some time for perfecting our mortal routines—after the big game, of course." Coach was ecstatic. The mustache hairs she'd missed shaving this a.m. actually stood up and quivered in delight.

Tara tried once more to talk sense into her. "Even if we can do just a little, we'll never get good enough for the Finals. We're witches. What do we know about lifting and throwing and jumping?"

"You'll be okay," I said before Coach could reply. "It only took me two months of hard work to figure everything out. And we have six months until Nationals."

I added, "Of course, Regionals are just before Christmas. And any team worth a tournament win competes in Regionals."

Although my probation status still hadn't been lifted, and my math had turned shaky, I suddenly felt safer than I had since I'd popped into the boys' locker room by mistake. I had something Coach wanted. Something the other girls wanted.

"Who wants to compete in Regionals? With mortals?" Tara asked the question in a way that dared anyone to raise a hand. She shouldn't have. I would have told her, if she'd asked me. But she didn't, because she thought she knew the answer.

Coach looked at the team. "Good question. Girls—raise your hand if you'd like to have a go at the national competition this year."

Every girl's hand went up—even the ones who were begging Tara with cringing puppy dog eyes to forgive them.

"Well, then. That's settled. Let's get to work."

Everyone looked from Tara to me, and I shivered. The look in the other girls' eyes was amazing. Part murderous, part worshipful.

I could live with it.

Chapter 15

ME: Remember the #3 routine last year?
Think CoachII mind if I do it here?
MADDIE: Of course Shed give birth 2 a brick
But whos gonna tell her? Nommee!
ME: K Then its #3 with mod
MADDIE: Mod? Kewl K

The routine was a simple one: lots of jumping, waving, and chanting letters—the stuff people expect from cheerleaders. Stuff the Salem cheerleaders needed to get them synchronized, which I knew would be my biggest problem if we weren't going to look like idiots at Regionals. But my secret weapon—to wow them all with my brilliance—was the extra moves.

Last year, with mortals, I chose to surprise the spectators with flip rolls. It's not a hard move, if you have two coordinated people, but it really wows the crowd.

It's a two-part trick. The way it goes, one person does a headstand and the other person does a backflip simultaneously, so that the flipper ends up facing the person doing the headstand. Next, the backflip person grabs the ankles of the other girl and does a dive roll through her legs. The headstander quickly grabs the flipper's ankles and rolls up to standing. The key is for both girls to hold on tight to her partner's ankles, so that they roll like a ball across the floor.

Coach liked the idea when I described it to her. The squad wasn't so sure, and given their coordination challenges, I didn't blame them. But my reputation was on the line, so I just smiled and broke them into teams of two to practice the move.

You'd think that witches would be more coordinated. But you'd be wrong. "No, you're supposed to grab her ankles, she grabs yours, and *then* you roll."

I'd never seen more fish flopping on the floor, not even the day we took my dad deep-sea fishing for his fortieth birthday.

"I think she's making fools of us. Mortals can't do this." Tara was clearly not going to give up without a fight.

"I can do it. It's the move that won us the tournament

last time." This was a calculated lie (mortals can do it, but it wasn't our winning move at Nationals). I needed Coach on my side, because without her, these girls were just never going to get behind getting in synch.

"Prove it." Tara had her hands on her hips, and her chin jutted out. She really didn't think I could do this. Which meant if I could, I'd be just this close to ending probation status.

Coach—I know she thought she was being helpful—said, "Actually, Tara, that's a good idea. A demonstration is just what these gals need. Go ahead, Prudence, show them your stuff."

I sweated bullets (even though I had deliberately orchestrated this challenge to prove my competence and make me elimination-proof for a little while—until I got my magic skills up to speed). The problem is, to do flip rolls you need a coordinated partner. Whom to choose when I didn't know who was standing there smiling, hoping I broke every bone in my body? Tara was one such squad member, of course. No doubt she had a stake in my failure since I was undermining her leadership big-time.

Coach, unfortunately, took my slight hesitation for a sign that I needed her help. "Tara, let her show you the move."

Great. I could see Tara wanted to sink her teeth into my big, juicy failure and send me from the team (maybe the school?) in tears and a sprinkling of black-and-blue fairy dust. No way José was I going to fail, even if I had to break every bone in *her* body.

"You do the headstand." I wasn't about to turn myself upside and down and present my ankles to her—I didn't want her to have the psych-out on me.

She did the headstand as if she were an eighty-year-old mortal with bad arthritis. Not that she couldn't handle it, just because she really didn't want to do anything I said—unless it was "Grab me around the throat and tighten until I turn blue and stop breathing."

I grasped her ankles firmly. "Grab hold of my ankles and grip tight."

She gripped like a really hungry boa constrictor. I could feel my toes turning numb.

"Not that tight. If my feet fall asleep, we're both in trouble."

She didn't let up, but I ignored her. My feet wouldn't fall asleep in the sixty seconds it would take to execute this maneuver and impress the heck out of these witches. Or not.

"Bow out." I pushed her hips to an outward bow, bent myself, and then started the roll. I sensed she was going to let go about a nanosecond before she did. Without thinking, I whispered,

"Fingers hold,
Fingers mold,

Tara to me,
Glue glue glue."

Beautiful? No. I never said my spell work was stellar, just becoming serviceable. I didn't even know if it would work. But over we went, with everyone's eyes pinned on us, I assume (I didn't know because I had my eyes firmly shut). We didn't come apart. We rolled around the room like a ball.

The dismount was a little rough. We were supposed to end up in the same position we'd started in, except with me in the headstand. As if I'd let that happen.

As soon as Tara countered my gripping spell—she'd been muttering under her breath since we started to roll—I let go. I heard her muttered chanting end with a breathless squeal. I hoped she was too disoriented to zap a wrist-burn spell on me.

Luckily, I landed on my feet while she managed to keep from flopping to the floor by levitating to the ceiling. I'm sure it helped her get rid of some frustration. Not that I had any sympathy.

Everyone clapped. In unison. At least there was one skill I wouldn't have to teach them for the competition. And I'd learned one skill of my own: I could cast a spell and still do a super-kewl move.

*

One thing I learned the day after my triumph at practice: Witches are just as mean as the meanest mortal girls. And they have more tricks up their sleeves.

Maybe if I hadn't shown up Tara, I wouldn't have been target du jour. But, just like back home, maybe I would have been, anyway. I do wish they hadn't messed with my lunch. I had skipped breakfast and I was hungry. Which meant I was meaner in response than I might have been. Which meant we ended up in the principal's office.

"Girls. I hear you're behaving like mortals." Agatha was no friendlier than she had been during my testing. But at least there were four of us in the room to divide the intensity of her glare.

Well, almost. She saved a special one for me. "I guess I can't expect more from you, Miss Stewart, since you were raised in the mortal realm." Somehow she made the word "mortal" sound like "worm." I didn't think that was a very positive sign.

Then she shifted her gaze to the other three and I realized she hadn't saved the worst for me. "But you girls! I expected better. Should I summon your parents?"

"No!" There was more unison in that answer than in any of their cheerleading moves. So they had potential. If they just dropped the chips off their shoulders—and didn't drop them on me.

"What happened?" Agatha ignored me and focused on Tara.

Tara shrugged. "She's just not very good at spells and she blames us."

"That's not true!" I protested.

"Miss Stewart, did I ask you to speak?"

"No."

"Then please do me the courtesy of controlling your mouth or I will have to lay a silencing spell upon you as if you were a two-year-old," said Agatha sternly.

The other girls tittered, like little blind mice following Tara's example. Sure, that's nice. Laugh at the half-blood girl in remedial classes.

"So, then," Agatha continued, turning back to Tara as if nothing had happened, "you had nothing to do with the incident in the lunchroom today?"

Maybe she wouldn't have gotten away with it if she'd just denied all involvement. But Tara was too diabolical for that. She looked down, as if she were sorry. Hah. "We were just trying to help. I swear."

Charity, Tara's right-hand nail polisher, broke in: "She conjured up this awful concoction for lunch that smelled so bad, it made us all gag. We just tried to help her by getting rid of it."

Right. Which was why the simple curry I'd been trying to conjure for lunch had turned into a tarry, gluey mass that stunk like twelve skunks and stuck to me in places that never saw the light of day. Who could blame me for sharing the joy with Tara and the other girls?

Agatha swallowed their explanation without an upraised eyebrow. "Thank you for being so honest with me, girls. I think this matter need go no farther. You may go."

For a moment, I was torn between protesting and slinking away, glad that this was going to disappear. Until Agatha said, "Please stay, Miss Stewart. We have more to discuss."

I'm sure I don't need to spell out the rest. The half-blood witch got a detention, while the bitch-witches got to skate. By the time I got home, I was ready to run away. Living on the streets of L.A. looked way better than sitting in a vat of mud for an hour tomorrow afternoon. Or facing the squad at practice the next day.

I could tell by the look on Mom's face that she'd been informed of the trouble. And the detention. So I didn't wait to hear what she had to say. "I renounce my witchness."

Dorklock stopped swigging milk straight from the carton to say, "That's like renouncing your blood type, stupid."

"Don't call me stupid," I snapped.

"You can't renounce your witchness, sweetie." Mom shocked me into speechlessness with her sympathy. I had gotten a detention! Me. The perfect daughter. And instead of grounding me, she was trying to console me! What she said next was even more shocking. "The most you can do is ask another witch to bind your powers. But that's an awfully drastic measure."

I hadn't really been serious. But suddenly it sounded like a plan. Get my powers bound and go to normal school. I could handle cheerleading there. No more remedial magic classes. "I'll do it! I'll bind my powers."

She hugged me. It was an awkward moment, because even though I just wanted to burrow up against her like I had when I was little, it was just not dignified. "I mean it."

"I'm sure you do, honey. But you can't bind your own powers. You need another witch to do it."

"Oh. You mean someone who has a Talent? Or maybe someone who has passed the Wisdom Test? Because I'm not seeing any Talent showing up. I'm going to be in remedial magic forever, and I have as much chance to make the team as a two-year-old does because that's how much magic I know. Why shouldn't I just give it all up?"

For a moment, I was tempted. If I weren't a witch, I wouldn't have to take the Wisdom Test, or any magic test ever again. Maybe I could move back–

Mom squeezed my hand. "It isn't the answer, no matter how tempting it seems. You *are* a witch, and you don't really know what that means yet. Maybe you should take it easy on yourself for a little while so you can find out."

"But it's so hard–" I began.

Mom interrupted before I could get into full-on harp mode. "Remember when you first started cheering and you fell off the top of a tower?"

"Not really. I blacked out."

"You know what I mean. For a few days you were convinced you'd never let anyone lift you off the ground ever again."

Okay. It was lecture time. It didn't make it better that she was right. "Fine. I'd rather fall off ten towers than be stuck in a vat of mud for an hour!"

"It's not so bad, if memory serves."

"You . . . ?" I stared at her, and she shocked me again—this time, by blushing. My mom, the almost-four-hundred-year-old witch, blushed. "Just pretend you're in an upscale spa."

I knew she was right. If I didn't show up at school tomorrow, that meant Tara had won. Frappiola. Sometimes life is not just unfair, it's triple-mega unfair. "Fine. But, remember, you promised if I don't manifest my Talent soon, you'd let me go live with Maddie."

"I remember." She was still sympathetic, but there was a little touch of worry there that I didn't like.

"Mom. If I—"

She sighed and held up her hand. "I hadn't wanted to mention this while you were still adjusting to life in Salem, but your Talent needs to manifest, Prudence, or there could be serious consequences."

"Like what? Will I sprout warts and a hairy chin?"

Mom didn't even crack a smile. "You could become mortal. Lose your powers."

"So?" Hadn't she heard a word I'd said about wanting to lose my powers?

"Witches who lose their powers that way usually get sick," she explained carefully.

"How sick?" I demanded. She didn't answer. Which was bad. Very bad. "Do they die?"

"Sometimes." Why couldn't I have a mom who would lie about something like that?

I didn't have anything to say to that. Even Dorklock didn't crack a joke. I guess he loved me after all. Or at least liked having me around to torment at will.

"Besides," Mom said, "I have good news. I've found Seamus. He's agreed to tutor you. We'll do a time-stretching spell this weekend so you can make the most of your study time."

For a minute I was actually happy. Maybe a little tutoring from an expert was all it would take to put the snap in my magic moves. But then I remembered Agatha's tone when she said the word "mortal." And the test she gave me when school started. Not to mention the fact she'd given me a detention and let Tara and the other girls flutter back to class without penalty of quicksand.

"Thanks, Mom. Now could you talk to Agatha for me? Because she hates me and I just know she has it in for me, even if Cousin Seamus *can* teach me what I need to know."

"That's not the positive Prudence I know."

Great. Mom had decided to turn on pep talk 101, about how focused I am when I want to be. I wish I could make violins play when she does that. Of course, being a magic no-nothing, I couldn't. I knew harps would play if I answered, so I just crossed my arms and dared her to pep me up.

"The Prudence I know tries her hardest."

Right. As if I haven't been trying my hardest since we landed in this frozen wasteland of witches who could fly rings around me—literally. But what was the point in saying it aloud? I just went to my room. To study. Sigh.

*

MADDIE: Who wants U off the team? Tell me
her name and Ill come kick her behind
ME: Tara the HC Shez mad cause Coach
likes me
MADDIE: Jealous much? Of course the coach
would favor U—U R a champion
ME: Coach is deluded if she thinks this team
has a chance at Regionals
MADDIE: Why?
ME: Our flyers R the best but we cant twirl in
sync Nervous Nellie shakes when she duz
a cartwheel and rolls like a drunken sailor
U never know where shell land
MADDIE: Is it ur coach?

ME: She doesnt get a lotta support from
the rents

MADDIE: Check Were lucky cause our rents
know cheerin can get U noticed by a producer
Guess in Salem thats not so likely

ME: These arent ur typical rents They dont
want models for kids

MADDIE: Oh Serious rents 2 bad 4 U

ME: Yeah A whole school full of rents like my
dad Not a pretty sight I almost feel lucky
Almost

MADDIE: What about the rest of the team?

ME: U tell me! Tara doesnt believe that jumps
and synchronization R important

MADDIE: 4 words Nair in the shampoo

ME: LOL!

MADDIE: Ull whipem into shape I know U
Gtg Date 2nite

ME: Date! Who? DT again?

There was no answer to my question, just silence. She was gone. It probably sounds funny, but when we text each other, it feels like she's there in my room. When we stop, though, there's just the little silver phone again.

I hate that feeling. But mostly I hated that my best friend was going out with a boy and I couldn't be there to help her

go through fifty dresses before she talked her mom into taking her to the store for just the right thing to wear on her
date. To find out all the dirt.

I hadn't even told her all my dirt. I'd been saving it for a
grand finish, but instead there was just the cold silver cell
that didn't care whether I had managed to earn myself a
detention in the first month of being at my new school
or not.

It didn't feel good. In fact, it felt like I'd lost my best
friend. For a minute, I considered bribing Dorklock to pop
me back in to Maddie's room so I could help her get ready
for this date of hers. I bet he could send me. For a price, of
course.

I even thought of the excuse I'd use to explain how I'd
turned up in California: a quick trip home to see my doctor for a sports physical. Mortals will fall for silly explana-
tions like that—they don't have powers and they don't really
believe in witches, except at Halloween.

But just then Dorklock barged in (without knocking . . .
without even opening the door, to be precise—he just stuck
his head through the door) to announce that Cousin
Seamus had arrived. I ended up practicing magic instead of
dishing with Maddie and making sure her makeup was just
right. I don't know if it would have made a difference if I'd
broken the rules and zapped myself to Beverly Hills.
Maybe. Maybe not.

*

Cousin Seamus wasn't nearly as old looking as I'd feared. He hadn't let his hair grow gray and, if my mom hadn't told me, I'd never have guessed he was older than twenty-five. He had that perennial young-man-on-the-verge-of-trouble look that so many of the boys in high school have. Which, as it turned out, made my tutoring session loads of fun.

"My motto is, if it doesn't make you laugh, why bother?" he began.

Sounded good to me. "I'm ready," I said, summoning my spell book.

"Does that make you laugh?"

I looked at the spell book. "It's just a book."

"Exactly." He gave it a tap, and it went spinning back to my room. "I prefer to use this." He pulled out his pockets, as if he were proving them empty to the cops. Glittery dust fell to the floor, swirled together for a moment, and formed into a little glittering iPod-like thing with legs and arms. Eyes opened on its iPod face and it examined me with a whirring, chirping sound that was nothing like laughter. Then, the little arms crossed over its squat middle.

"Give her a chance, Toot." Seamus tapped the top of his magic gadget. "You know her mother's been living a mortal life for twenty years—and she's dragged the kids into it too."

Toot made a few more squeals and beeps, then uncrossed his arms. All of a sudden, he pushed a button on his side and projected three objects in the air: a red ball, a blue cube, and a banana—yellow, of course.

He waited, tapping the foot of one of his glittery legs.

I could see from Cousin Seamus's solemn expression that this was a test. But a test of what? How crazy was my mother to think I could learn anything from these two? And, oh joy, in time-stretching mode at that.

I reached out for the objects, surprised that they were solid. I started juggling them. Slowly. We'd done some juggling for a routine two years ago, but I was rusty.

And then I decided I had nothing to lose. I juggled them with my magic rather than my hands. As they juggled through the air, I used all my concentration to unpeel the banana. And then, letting everything else drop to the ground, I ate the banana.

They still didn't seem impressed, so I said, "Show me food, and I'll eat it."

Toot laughed by bending in half and slapping his knee.

My cousin giggled. "She has potential, Toot." His giggle was weird, but by the end of our time-stretched tutoring, I'd learned to enjoy it. After all, it meant I'd gotten the equivalent of an A from a very hard taskmaster.

You'd think that a lesson that required laughter would be easy. You'd be wrong. But I have to say that I learned more in the session of tutoring with Cousin Seamus than I'd learned in three weeks of remedial spells.

Of course, he just laughed when I said, "You know, I must be ready to pass the Wisdom Test by now." I'd gotten to know him well enough to know that was the laugh that meant I'd said something truly stupid. But even if I wasn't ready for the Wisdom Test, I *was* ready to get into regular magic classes. And maybe cheer in a game against a magic school.

Don't laugh. I was exhausted, and my natural optimism was overtaking my common sense. It only took a good night's sleep to remind me I was definitely not in Kansas anymore.

Chapter 16

ME: Big date news?
MADDIE: Sokay
ME: Not good?
MADDIE: Nuff said bout me U got the big
game Luck

Maddie didn't know the half of it. Trying for the best in mortal cheering wasn't the easiest thing in the world. It's not just prancing around and looking pretty like some people think. You have to trust one another, and you have to catch one another, even when your flyer can't stand the sight of her bases or vice versa. If you don't, bones get broken, heads get knocked, and competitions get lost.

Watching the football game between Agatha's and the Washington Black Arts, I suddenly understood why Tara gave me pitying smiles and got annoyed with Coach's interest in mortal competition. My first witch game was a pom-pom-shredding experience. I only wish I could have shared it with Maddie. She'd have been impressed, just like I was.

Lots of previously mysterious things were explained—like why the varsity cheerleaders were sloppy with their floor moves. Witch cheers are not done on the floor. Too tame. Everything is done in the air. By the time I'd watched both squads spin, twist, twirl, and fly through the air, I'd realized I was very lucky to have made even a probational spot on the varsity squad. Not that I'd admit it in a million, zillion years.

I sat on the bench that game. Water girl extraordinaire. But I watched and I learned and I noticed something important: There wasn't a lot of synchronization among either squad—the kind of synchronization that makes a squad look not only impressive, but like one unit. My old coach had stressed the importance of that until our ears rang with words like "Together!" and "Timing, people!"

I had something to offer. They just didn't know it yet. With proper timing, the awesome air routines would become triple awesome. Not to mention less dangerous. I saw at least five cheerleaders collide in midair and get pulled back to the bench by the coaches. And not just the inexperienced or the not very good cheerleaders. Tara got hurt flying into one of the players because she had to avoid a quick dip and flip from a girl on the other squad.

Coach gave her an ice pack and sat her on the bench next to me. Joy.

"Ready to run home to mortal school yet?" she sneered at me.

"It's impressive," I admitted. Everyone likes a compliment. "Just like that shiner you're going to have tomorrow."

"Some people shouldn't be allowed to fly." She glared at the flyer who had hit her—who was still a risk to those flying around her.

"Yeah. Most people don't get how challenging mortal cheerleading is. This stuff is definitely high-octane risk."

"Well, at least you know you're out of your league and didn't beg to go in. I don't know what her excuse is."

"You know, if you coordinated your moves, even the high-speed, midair stuff would be safer—and would look better too," I said tentatively.

"What do *you* know?" She'd abandoned the cheerleader smile—probably because it hurt. Apparently scowling at me also hurt, because she winced and pressed the ice pack more tightly against her face.

"I know that synchronization isn't a dirty word—on the floor or in the air."

"Oh, get over yourself. *NSYNC is dead and so are you."

"You will be, too, if you get hit by another cow in the air."

"I'll take care of her." She moved her pinkie, just the barest twitch, and the clumsy flyer tumbled into the stands. Not an approved move, even for witch school.

"If someone catches you—"

"No one ever does." She clutched her ice pack, eyes closed, looking the picture of helplessness as everyone scanned the court for the culprit.

Clumsy Cow was screaming something about evil magic from across the way, but since she'd sidelined Tara and two of her own squad, I guess the coaches weren't interested in finding out who had saved the rest of them from injury.

"One day that nasty temper of yours is going to come back and bite you," I said, shaking my head in awe.

"Right. And one day you won't be in remedial magic class. Keep telling yourself that if it gives you hope, sweetie."

I was spared trying to out-nasty the Queen of Nasty because halftime ended and the flyers dove back to the bench, exuberant from being center stage. I missed that feeling. There is nothing like it. I hoped that the next time we played a magic team, I'd be ready to go out on the field with the squad. And I wouldn't let anyone run into me.

To that end, I called on Prudence, Queen of the Type A's, and made Tara an offer she couldn't refuse: "What if I show you how synchronization could improve your air work and your floor work?"

"You can't even do air work," Tara replied, sounding bored.

"What would it take for you to let me show you?"

Her narrow little eyes said nothing. And then, as if she'd been smacked on the bottom by Mr. Phogg, she got the "lightbulb on" look. "Is it true you have a car?"

Chapter 17

"Hey, 666 Girl, I hear you survived your first witches-only game." Daniel caught me just as I was going into the cafeteria. Right as I stepped into the room, the doors swinging open before me—and staying open as he snapped his fingers, grinned at me, and everything stopped except us.

You know how, in mortal movies, they try to capture that moment when time seems to stop? They do a pretty good job of it, because the movie time-stop is pretty much like real time-stopping.

I could see Daniel grinning at me, moving toward me. I could see outside the circle of us, where Tara and the other cheerleaders were stopped cold, mid-whatever. Interestingly, the whatever did not seem to include eating. One was putting on mascara, two were looking up at Tara, and three were talking to one another, tuning Tara out. I could so relate.

I looked at Daniel, who had that bad-boy gleam in his eye. As usual. I ignored the pull I felt toward him and stopped walking. I wanted him to think I was cool. He probably guessed I had a crush, but I didn't have to confirm it by acting easy. "Weird. How did you do that?" I would have asked him why, but it seemed obvious—because he could.

"You said you couldn't be alone with me without breaking into hives. And I didn't think you'd let me kiss you in the hallway in front of everyone. Plus, the little witch's room has an unbreakable warding spell keyed to all males, even rats and mice."

"So." I tried to smile seductively, but I may have just come off as nervous. He was a clever, clever boy. He hadn't broken my mother's spell, he'd found a way around it. "Do you think I'm the kind of girl who'll kiss you in public?"

"Don't know. Don't care. So long as you're a girl who'll kiss me in a time bubble with no one looking but us."

He leaned toward me, and our lips touched. His were warm, mine were surprisingly compressible. He flicked my lip with his tongue, and I shivered. "How much trouble are we going to get in for this?"

He kissed me again, lightly. "If they catch us? Detention. Or maybe they'll expel us."

For some reason, when Daniel said it, being expelled sounded like a good thing. Or maybe it was just the effect of the time bubble, magnifying everything I felt standing there kissing him without having to worry about my sixty-second limit. I leaned into him for another kiss.

He grinned. "Some things you don't learn in school, hunh?"

"Like what?"

"Like kisses aren't supposed to end quickly." Our mouths pressed together for my first ever longer-than-sixty-second kiss. At last. It was wonderful.

And then, all hell broke lose. Figuratively, but in a literal way too. The bubble around us started to glow, alarms sounded, and a big flash of flame and smoke drove us apart—and deposited Agatha between us.

I don't know what I hoped for, except, of course, to disappear, which I had not yet learned to do on purpose (definitely not a remedial skill—the teachers would hate having to look for students all the time).

I quickly decided on my course of action: I'd plead innocent. I opened my mouth, but one quick jab of Agatha's finger and I couldn't speak.

"Daniel. I know this is all her fault. You just had to impress an empty-headed female again, didn't you," she snapped.

My fault? Empty-headed? Again? I would have said . . . if I could have talked.

"G. Don't get so bent out of shape." Daniel was grinning at Agatha as if she were not still wafting a chilly mist from the folds of her robes—and maybe from her nostrils, too, it was hard to tell.

"Don't 'G' me, young man. I've warned you. You have to tread the straight and narrow. Your family legacy is not one of brigandage and rule breaking."

"G, that's not for me. I've told you before—"

At that moment, a horrible monkey-screeching sound drowned out anything Daniel had to say.

When the sound stopped, both Agatha and Daniel looked worried. "They're coming," Agatha said, her words releasing two little puffs of steam into the air.

"You'd actually expel me for this?" He didn't look happy, especially when the loud screeching came again, this time accompanied by what sounded like a flapping of wings. Big wings.

"A time bubble in school is an automatic expulsion hearing. I can't do anything about it. You've gone over the line now, Daniel. Our bloodline can only protect you so far."

Our bloodline? Hold up. Were they related? Is that what 'G' meant—Grandma?!

He shrugged, but I could see a bit of worry in his eyes as the screeching sounded again, closer this time. Then he grinned, kissed Agatha on her wrinkled cheek, said, "Catchya later, 666 Girl," and disappeared. As the monkey screech started again, and the bubble began to dissolve around us, words appeared in the air. "You can't expel me, G. I quit!"

Agatha and I suddenly stood under the watchful eyes of all the other students as the horrible screaming things arrived. They not only sounded like monkeys, they looked like monkeys. Those evil winged monkeys from *The Wizard of Oz* that scared me off the couch and into Mom's lap when I was three. You know, the ones that almost ate Toto.

They came at us with sharp claws stretched and reaching. Or rather they came at me, because Agatha was head-mistress and Daniel was . . . gone.

I couldn't help it: They were scary. I screamed. Nothing came out, which may, in the end, have saved my life . . . or at least one of my limbs.

Agatha stopped the marauding monkeys one nanosecond before they reached me. I swear one of the lead monkey's claws left a faint scratch on my chin.

"Leave her. I'll deal with her," she commanded.

The monkeys weren't happy, or so their lower decibel, but still ear-blasting, screeches indicated.

"She isn't eligible for immediate expulsion." Agatha didn't sound completely happy about that. "Miss Stewart didn't cast the spell. She couldn't tie her shoelaces with magic, and she certainly couldn't conjure a time bubble. I'll hold a regular hearing at the school and inform you of our decision." Agatha didn't wait to hear out the protests. She just whisked me away to her office.

"Why couldn't you just leave him alone?" A frosty mist was coming thick and heavy from her robes. "He was doing so well this time."

Okay. So Agatha apparently had a big-time blind spot for her great-to-the-nth-power grandson. Who hadn't mentioned that Agatha was G, his great-great-great-great-grandmother. Where was the rumor mill when I needed it most?

I considered how to answer. But I couldn't think of a single thing that would make her see Daniel as anything more than an innocent in the grip of a scheming female. Apparently that charm of his worked on girls from sixteen to sixteen hundred, and there wasn't any getting around it.

There was really only one question. I hadn't meant to ask it, but as soon as Agatha gave me back my power of speech, I did. "Are you going to expel me?" It was scary how much of me hoped the answer was yes. As long as I didn't have to deal with those monkeys ever again.

Agatha frowned at me. "We'll discuss that when your parents get here."

Great.

Chapter 18

Once I was home and safe in my room, I turned on my phone to call Maddie. I was grounded, of course. I didn't know whether I would be expelled, have my powers bound, or get a big, fat scarlet L—for loser—to wear on my forehead. And, really, I didn't care.

I mean, if Daniel could run away, why couldn't I? The Dorklock would pop me to Beverly Hills if I asked him. And I had over two hundred dollars in savings that I could spend on gas to drive there if Tobias suddenly decided he'd had enough troublemaking.

The phone beeped in my hand to indicate I had a message.

Look whos canoodlin

I hadn't heard from Maddie in a while, but with the detention, the game, and Cousin Seamus, I hadn't made much effort to contact her, either. So when the message came in with a picture, it took a minute to realize it wasn't from Maddie. It was from someone else—someone who had masked the incoming number. I sensed trouble, but what was new? Since I'd been in Salem, I'd been a trouble magnet.

The picture on my cell phone was of Maddie and Brent. Holding hands.

No wonder she hadn't been text messaging me much. She had a way guilty conscience.

I hid the phone under my pillow and blew off steam by creating a little tornado in the center of my room. Neat trick Cousin Seamus taught me to get rid of excess anger so I didn't do anything stupid in school and earn myself another detention. Hah! The tornado, he said, comes and goes without permanent disruption of anything. Unfortunately, it also did not disrupt the questions shooting through my mind. Why was Maddie dating a boy she knew I liked? Well, maybe I knew the answer to that one. But, then, why hadn't she just told me? I would have understood. I think.

I had to see Maddie. The problem, of course, was that I could not pop myself more than three feet yet. And even that skill was spotty. Asking my mother to pop me to

Beverly Hills—especially after being caught in a time bubble with a boy and facing a possible expulsion—would be more trouble than it was worth. Not to mention that it would raise questions that would last longer than the echo of her very definite no. I didn't want her to know about Maddie and Brent. Or how much it hurt.

I'd been scared when the monkeys were flying at me, and highly annoyed with Daniel for leaving me to face the consequences alone. But seeing Maddie and Brent in a clinch? My heart just squeezed up into a hard ball thinking about it. How could she? We'd been friends forever. Best friends. Why hadn't she told me? I had to know.

I thought of asking Samuel for help, but again, questions that might reveal my lingering crush on a mortal boy seemed like dangerous territory. He'd send me, but he'd want me to come back. And I wasn't sure I could do that. Even if Maddie turned out to be my best enemy, I wasn't ready to face the humiliation at Agatha's after what had happened.

There was really only one choice. True, it was a horrible choice, but it was the only one I had. So I asked the Dorklock to send me to Beverly Hills. And I offered the only bribe that I knew would work: I told him I would take the blame for his next big goof-up.

Being the Dorklock, he tried to bargain me up to two goof-ups. But I refused, countering with the stipulation that

I would take the blame for his next *big* goof-up, not any-thing minor. Not that I really cared. But I didn't want him to get suspicious. I hadn't told him that I didn't know if I *would* come back, so I'd had to make the bargaining look good, even though my heart wasn't in it.

So that's how I found myself back at Beverly Hills High School on a bonfire night. I stood there a minute, just watching the crackling fire. I'd always loved bonfire night. If things had been different, I might have been there with Brent. Although, to be fair, maybe I'd have been there with someone else. Boy-girl stuff is unpredictable in high school, be it mortal high school or witch high school.

I'd attempted a bit of a disguise: a cute but shapeless sweatshirt and a ball cap I'd never be caught dead wearing otherwise. The last thing I needed was for someone to rec-ognize me and tell Maddie I was there before I could find her myself. I had to know if the picture was real. Or if some-one with a grudge against me had doctored it to do a little long-distance torturing.

Turned out the distance wasn't so bad. It hurt much worse to see them in the flesh.

Maddie was there. With Brent. They were only a few feet away, turned toward the bonfire, arms wrapped around each other. No way was this a first date. I remembered how she had stopped telling me about Danny Trimball and had just let me think she was still seeing him. When all along, she'd been with Brent, not saying a word to me about it.

I felt my hurt and anger rush through me like an inferno. For a microsecond, I was distracted, wondering whether I had a Fire Talent. But who cared? All I cared about was the sight of my best friend hugging my boy. I couldn't wait to see what she would have to say when she saw me. The rat.

I waited for her to turn and catch sight of me. I was sure she'd recognize me, even if no one else did. We were best friends. We *had* been best friends forever.

I stood there for what seemed like so long, I could have been in one of Daniel's time bubbles. The bonfire burned down, couples started to drift away, and the teachers went around breaking up those who had gotten too wrapped up in their darkness-enhanced make-out sessions to notice it was time to go.

I heard Maddie laugh and Brent lean down to whisper in her ear as they turned toward me. It was dark, but I knew she'd know me. If only she'd look at me instead of up at Brent.

Chezzie brushed by them, her newest boyfriend on her arm. I didn't recognize him, but Maddie had said he was the football captain and had transferred in from somewhere else. "Better be careful Pru doesn't come by for a surprise visit, Maddie."

Maddie laughed again. She didn't even have the decency

to look ashamed. "Pru is happy in Salem, Chezzie. She's got a new car, a new squad, and a new boyfriend." And then she looked right at me.

I don't know if I was more angry that she could say something that was so opposite of the truth—that she might not know me well enough to know it *wasn't* the truth—or more afraid that when our eyes met, I'd know that I'd lost my best friend. But I never had a chance to find out which was worse. Because when she looked at me, she didn't react. Worse, she—and Brent—walked right by me as if I weren't there. Because, technically, I wasn't.

It took me a second to realize that I had turned invisible—involuntarily—for the first time in six years. Invisible. So I'd seen Maddie, but she hadn't seen me.

I let her walk away, arm in arm with Brent. The irony of the fact that she was wearing the cute jacket she'd borrowed from me sometime last fall was not lost on me.

I debated running after her, despite the fact that my feet seemed planted to the ground. But what would I ask her? Why she hadn't told me she was seeing Brent? Or whether I could sleep in her closet for the next year and a half so I didn't have to go home to my loser life in Salem?

I was still debating when Mom popped in behind me, busting me big-time. I confess, I'd never been so glad to be busted in my life.

"Prudence," she started, just as if she could see me.

I ran at her and wrapped my arms around her. "Mom, I don't belong anywhere now." Then I started to cry. I didn't stop for a long time, even after we were safely back in Salem.

I think Mom was planning to ground me some more, maybe lecture my ears off. But I was such a mess, she didn't have the heart to do it. She just held me tight and whispered, over and over, "It's hard right now. I know, honey. But it *will* get better. It will."

I tried to believe her. And then, when that failed, I tried to act like I believed her. But nothing helped.

Dad started to go into "Rambo Lecture" mode when we popped back into the kitchen. But Mom just shook her head and they stood together, arm in arm, like Maddie and Brent had been, while I climbed the stairs to my room.

Even the Dorklock left me alone. Although that might have been because Mom was grounding him every way possible for his part in my crime. Whatever. I was just glad to be left alone.

I sat on my bed, in my Rapunzel tower, wondering if Rapunzel had regretted leaving with the prince. I put my fingers on the red streaks on my bedspread and, holding my breath, zapped them away. My bedspread was as good as new. No memories left.

I pulled my cell phone out and checked the picture again. Yep. Maddie and Brent. You expect people who don't like you to be a beeyotch to you. But your best friend?

I printed the picture—a good, clear eight-by-ten, which made the crime so much worse. Maddie was smiling that "I'm so happy" smile. Her makeup was a little off—she always overdoes the eye shadow if I'm not there to stop her.

I got out my candles and lit them. A good zit spell was just what she deserved. My hands were shaking as I paged through the book. I knew there had to be one—there were anti-zit spells thousands of years old.

The tears in my eyes made it hard to read, but I refused to give up. At last, I found it.

Hie! And Fie! And Fickle Skin.
Raise red welts, and puss within.
Time and money can't defeat.
The blemish'd soul shows upon the skin.

Not the most elegant spell, but I guess whoever had written it had been too angry for elegance. I could so relate.

I looked at the picture and wiped away my tears. "There are advantages to being a witch, Maddie." And I was glad, for the first time, that there were.

I wished I could see her face when she woke up in the morning. On second thought, who'd want to look at that gross thing? Not me. And I hoped not Brent.

I touched Maddie's clear face in the picture. "Some

things are sacred, Maddie. I thought you knew that."

Mom knocked softly. "Prudence, do you have the book? I need it."

I swept away the picture so she wouldn't see it and I quickly flipped the book to a random page. Mom wouldn't approve of zit spells. Not even for boyfriend stealers. She was like that.

"Here it is—" I closed the book and started to get up to hand it to her. But then I stopped and zapped it to her.

She blinked for a second, as if she was surprised. "What's gotten into you?"

"Might as well live like a witch, now that we've joined the better witch club of Salem."

I'm pretty sure she thought of several things to say to me before she settled on, "Things will get easier, honey. You're such a hard worker. Have I told you recently how proud I am of you?"

"I like straight A's." For a minute, we both pretended that I was still a straight-A student, a head cheerleader, and not a loser. "I guess this witch stuff isn't so bad."

Sometimes it could be downright good, as a matter of fact. I crushed the photo behind my back and zapped it into oblivion. After all, Beverly Hills was dead to me now. Forever.

Chapter 19

When I got back to school, it was almost an anticlimax to find out that I'd gotten a week's worth of detentions for not bursting Daniel's time bubble right away. Big surprise. Well, actually, it was. I had thought, given my recent dive into the depths of the unlucky, that I'd get kicked out of Agatha's just when I had no place to go back to in Beverly Hills.

For a second, I was almost happy with mere detention. But I should have known Agatha wasn't as forgiving as she seemed in front of my parents. No. She went to Coach Gertie to try to get my probational status revoked. Coach had said no. So far, Agatha hadn't tried any other indirect punishment. But I knew enough about Agatha to know that her wrath was like a giant iceberg. Only the tip showed. I'd have to watch my back for any sudden chills.

No one said a word to me when we popped into our lockers the next morning. Even Samuel didn't say anything sympathetic when I offered him the half a brownie Hi hadn't wanted. Okay. Apparently he was choosing to believe the rumor that Daniel and I had done more than kiss in that time bubble.

Which meant I needed to get Samuel back on my side again. I'd already lost my quota of friends for the year. And, oddly enough, the idea of losing Samuel as tutor buddy and mortal groupie made me want to cry. Again. I might have, if I wasn't already drained dry. So I pulled out the big guns. I lured him back for one more tutoring session by leaning in and saying, "I have a favor to ask when you come to tutor tonight." I said it right before we popped out of the hallway and into our first classes, so he couldn't answer. I trusted curiosity—and that pesky crush of his—would ensure he showed. Fortunately, I was right.

"You want me to do what? For whom?" Samuel flipped his lenses at me, as if maybe looking at me in another dimension would change what I had said. Fat chance. With Maddie and Beverly Hills dead to me, I needed to make it here even more than I had before.

"I told you. I want to be head cheerleader at Agatha's next year. Which means I need to make Tara my friend now."

"I'm not a Magic Hacker, I'm an Earth Talent, Pru."

"Right. And a powerful one too. If you can't get around a few location spells, I don't know who can."

He seemed alternately pleased and horrified that I thought so highly of his skills, and that I had finally begun to catch on to the magic stuff enough to ask him to stretch his skills to the breaking point.

"Look, if you can't hack a few spells so we can play hooky, maybe I'll just have to ask someone else." Not, of course, that there was anyone else to ask now that Daniel had gone for good (although rumor had it that Agatha was doing the big search thing and all would be forgiven—again—if she found him).

Apparently this hadn't escaped Samuel's notice either. "I'm sure Daniel would have done it for you if he hadn't run away."

"Daminee, all he did was try to show me how to get around my mom's anti-kissing spell. And the monkeys made sure I didn't even get to find out if it would have worked." Oops. I told the white lie to save his ego. But I shouldn't have said anything of the kind to Samuel. Because I could see the next thing out of his mouth would be . . .

"That's because he tried a time bubble. It was bound to set off the sensors. He's such a show-off. If you want to get around that anti-kissing spell, I can show you."

Right. Seems like a great idea . . . unless you don't want

Samuel suggesting that he test out the success of his spell with a little lip-lock between friends. Between Maddie and Daniel—and two weeks' detention—I'm so over that right now. "I'll figure it out on my own."

The thing I hate most about Samuel is that he's no dummy. He was hurt. "Fine. If I'm not good enough to show you the anti-kissing spell, you can figure out the skipping-school spell on your own, too, then."

Great. I had lost Maddie, and now I was about to lose Samuel. I considered wringing out just a few more tears, but then realized that crying wasn't likely to make Samuel anything but squirmy. He was a boy, even though I sometimes forgot it. So, instead, I said, "Can't you give me a break? I've had a hard couple of days." I'd told him about Maddie.

"Sorry. I just don't like to think I'm being used."

"Are you kidding? You're the only friend I have left in this world right now." I'd said it to reassure him. But suddenly I realized it was true. Somewhere in the midst of sharing curry and chocolate cake, tutoring, and trading mortal tidbits, we'd become friends. I trusted Samuel like I used to trust Maddie. Completely. "I just don't want to wreck our friendship with any—well, you know."

"Okay." But he hadn't lost hope, I could tell, because instead of flipping me off and leaving, he immediately said, "You skipped school in your old school, didn't you?"

"Yes. But we only had security cameras and security

guards to fool—not binding spells and teachers so old, they not only know every trick in the book, they know the counterspell as well. Besides, I have to do it well enough not to get caught. I can't afford another detention. And if I get Tara into trouble, that will be the end of making nice with the head cheerleader."

Samuel nodded. "Tara will roast you alive if you get her a detention."

"But she'll owe me if I don't." I had suspected that taking Tara on a hooky drive in my car would be the way to her heart ever since I saw her knock that clumsy girl off the court with a switch of her little finger.

"True." I was surprised at how quickly he replied. Even I wasn't as certain as Samuel sounded.

"How do you know?" I wondered for a brief, absurd moment if they'd ever dated.

But, no. "I listen."

Of course he does. If he weren't my friend, I'd be very, very nervous of Samuel's listening skills.

"You'll do it? For me? I'll give you my cell phone." After all, I didn't need it now that I wasn't talking to Maddie. But I didn't tell him that.

He looked thoughtful for a minute. "Okay. But I get to come with." He took the cell phone and, as good as his word, I made the first step toward binding Tara to me in friendship.

*

Okay, maybe not a friendship, exactly. More like an alliance. One where, when I told her Samuel was coming along, she had to bring someone extra too. So on Monday morning, there were four of us instead of three in the bright yellow Jetta: Samuel, Tara, and her #2 on the squad, Charity. Oh, and little old me, who was praying that none of us got caught by the magic police, bumped into another car by accident, or ran out of gas before we got safely back from our out-of-school experience.

"I want to see Rodeo Drive." Charity was a good cheer-leader, but she didn't have a clue about the mortal world. I think it was her absolute lack of fear that she would mess up that made her a great flyer—and a lousy person to take with me on the day I skipped school.

"That's in California," I explained patiently.

"Okay." She made as if to zap us there, and I blocked the spell (those sessions with Cousin Seamus had really paid off). "Hey. I said I'd take you for a drive around the neighborhood, not the world. You promised no magic." Like I said, she was totally clueless. But Tara didn't go anywhere without Charity by her side. They were like night and day. Power Girl, full of dark, mean thoughts, and Clueless Girl, light and fluffy and fearlessly cheerful.

Samuel muttered under his breath. I knew he thought I was going to owe him big time.

Charity persisted. "Just a little—to get us to Rodeo Drive."

"No. I'm going to drive us. We can go to the mall, if you want. The Salem Mall."

"The mall is good. If we get caught . . ." Tara was nervous. Wow. Hadn't she ever skipped school before? Well, of course not. Only Samuel had managed to combat all the binding spells our parents had put on us, and he'd needed help from Tara the Magic Talent and Charity the Water Talent to do it.

Charity pouted, which I guess must have worked for her parents, but it was three against one and even though my blocking skills were poor, Samuel was a whiz.

"Can't you go any faster?" Tara leaned forward and glanced around (she was riding shotgun, of course). I couldn't tell whether she was loosening up—or trying to get her big adventure over with just a tiny bit faster.

I shook my head. "I could if I had the Mercedes. But in this, the best I can do is seventy-five." Not that my dad wouldn't have a cow if he ever found out.

Samuel leaned forward. "I could juice up the engine—" The next thing he'd be offering to do was drive. As if.

"No, thank you. My mother has put so many spells on this car, it isn't funny." Sometimes your parents do something that gives you an insight into what they're afraid of. Frankly, after my mom listed the anti-carjacking spell, the anti-hydroplaning spell, and the little spell to keep tree limbs from falling on my car, I was afraid to ask what else she'd done. Sometimes, knowing how much she tries to protect me, I wonder why she moved us to Salem.

But it doesn't really matter. I'm here now. I've got Samuel in my corner and Tara starting to see that I could be a useful ally.

Coach nearly dropped her whistle when Tara and I came in together to ask if we could work on getting the team synchronized in preparation for the regional and national competitions.

"I'm so glad you understand how important this can be for us." She was talking to Tara, but her smile was for me. Coach Gertie was no dummy. I thought of all the classes of girls she'd coached at the school, and I realized she probably knew more about what was going on in our heads than we did. Scary.

"We want to do it for you, Coach," Tara said, in good cheerleader-suck-up form.

I thought, for one crazy moment, that Coach Gertie was going to hug us. Fortunately, she recovered her whistle and gave three shrill blows of joy instead.

"Girls! Listen up. We're going to get in shape for Regionals starting today."

The rest of the team was not so happy. Especially when I explained how precise we'd have to be to do well. But you know what they say about telling, showing, and doing: Doing always wins.

"I just want everyone to see the difference. If I could have two volunteers?" Naturally, everyone looked at Tara, not trusting the sudden favor she seemed to be bestowing on the girl she'd tried to sabotage not that long ago. No one volunteered.

"Choose two, Prudence." Great. Coach had put me in a lose-lose position.

But I'd beaten worse odds before. "Brunhilda and Celestina, come on down." I'd heard them talking about *The Price Is Right* at lunch, so I hoped they'd laugh. They did. But they didn't move. Not so good.

Coach prodded them with her whistle and the promise of benching if they didn't participate.

"I don't see why we should have to be held back to mortal restrictions." Brunhilda had manifested an Air Talent, so she was book smart, as mortals say. But not people smart—or, in this case, witch smart. As cheerleaders go, she was of average abilities. But as witches go, she could fly circles around the eagles. That's why I needed her. That and the fact that she was not in Tara's tight circle. Rumor had it that she'd been kicked out when she dared admit she had a crush on a boy Tara considered hers. At least last year, anyway.

As for Celestina, she was tiny and nearly invisible until

she put on her uniform. But she had rhythm. And that was critical to this demonstration.

I'd listened to a little locker room talk. Enough to know what would push them. They had the usual love-hate relationship with the head cheerleader. So I knew what they were thinking, even if they were keeping their game smiles in place: *Tara would hate for us to do well at competition. Then we'd all have to shine instead of just her.* Which was true, despite the fact that Tara had agreed to work with me on synch. I'm no dummy when it comes to girl-olotics. She'd agreed because I have a car and she doesn't—and because she hoped that I'd fail miserably with my mortal techniques so that she was once more the unchallenged queen of the squad.

Which meant it was my job to make the team look great in the air, and on the ground, without taking any of the shine from Tara's crown. Call me crazy, but I was up for the challenge. "We're going to win Nationals on our first try—if we do what we need to do." I looked at the girls, who were watching me carefully. They liked what I was saying, but that didn't mean they believed it. Yet. I looked over at Tara. If she wanted us to shine, it was her turn.

I could see she knew it. She put all her pizzazz into leading the cheer. "Let me hear you say it. Go Witches! Win Nationals!"

They weren't quite as enthusiastic as I needed them

to be when they cheered in unison, "Go Witches! Win Nationals!" But that would change. Competition was like that. When it's them against us, us forgets who flirted with whose boyfriend or hogged the mirror right before a game.

I finished with the cherry on top. I pulled out some Scharffen Berger chocolate I'd been saving since our last trip to San Francisco. They fell on it like a pack of starving wolves. Back home, they'd have run into the rest room to barf it up. In witchworld, they just patted their stomachs and lined up to follow my lead.

It took three bruised shins (two mine) and one ice pack to the head (not mine), but we did it. We showed the girls that an air routine could be cooler, and safer, when everyone followed the timing of the music and stayed synchronized with one another. We hadn't done much, just a few air buckets and some flying V's. But I could see the girls got it.

Tara got it too. To ward off her evil eye, I didn't need magic, just a little quick crown polishing. When Coach Gertie started praising me, I thanked Tara for being an insightful and forward-thinking head cheerleader, to see how this could take the squad beyond school games. By the end of my little speech, even Coach Gertie had begun to think it was all Tara's idea to use my expertise to take the team to Nationals.

I crown-polished but good, and I'm not ashamed of it in the least. I wanted shared custody of the credit—and the blame—with Tara. She was head cheerleader, after all. And I'd rather head off any schemes she was working on to get me off the team for good. After a lifetime of being on Team Us in Beverly Hills, I wanted to be part of Team Us at Agatha's, even if it meant doing it Salem-style.

But it wasn't until the end of practice that day that I finally got my reward.

When Coach Gertie blew her whistle twice to end practice, she gathered us all in and exchanged a smile with Tara. "Girls, congratulate Prudence. She is no longer on probation. She is a full member of our team."

The girls waited until Tara clapped me on the back so hard, I thought I'd never breathe again. Then they surrounded me with girlie squeals and jumping hugs.

So, to recap the short, not-so-sweet life of Prudence Stewart: Yep, it's official. Life is not fair. Picture glowing letters about ten inches high—in red, black, and orange, my new school colors. I'm one month into my new and unimproved life as a witch in Salem. My best friend since preschool didn't even wait until my seat on the bus had cooled before she made a move on the guy she knew I liked. The cutest, baddest boy in school left me in the middle of the cafeteria to face the music for our one short kiss. I still have to deal with Skin and Bones and remedial magic classes. Not to mention boys, or the million-zillion daily things that can go wrong for any sixteen-year-old witch who still has to manifest her Talent, study magic until her nose turns purple, and find a boy to take her to school dances.

But so what? I can deal. After all, I have Samuel, the remedial student's secret weapon for getting into regular classwork faster than the speed of light. I have the car Grandmama gave me. And I have the inside scoop on outside cheering competitions. Most important, I made it. I'm on the team, and I'm off probation. I have a squad to get my back when the mismixed potion hits the fan.

One thing I know for sure is that no matter how unfair life is, everything works out better when you have a great cheering squad to make sure you keep those moves tight, sharp, and in perfect form. Not to mention catch you when you fall, even if it's just a half second before you land on your face.

Don't miss out on the magic
in Pru's next adventure:
Competition's a Witch

Is it really so awful that I sometimes look to the mortals in my life for a little break from the hot and heavy magic? Sometimes it's good to spend some time with people who aren't comparing their summoning or potion skills to yours.

Take yesterday, for example, and my introduction to the cutest boy in Salem, witch or mortal. He'd come in tow behind his mother, who had made him carry the big welcome-to-the-neighborhood casserole she'd cooked up for us. At first I didn't even notice he was more than cute, because his mother was one of those annoyingly bigger-than-life people who suck all the oxygen out of a room the second they start to speak.

Which she did, as soon as my mother opened the door. "Welcome to the neighborhood. I'm sorry it has taken me so long to get over and give you a proper welcome, but my husband and I took a little vacation to France to celebrate our anniversary and we're just now back."

Mom just stood there, looking like she wished she hadn't opened the door wide enough that the neighbor had been able to walk right into the living room and start assessing our stuff from floor to ceiling. "Thank you. But you didn't have to—"

"Nonsense. No one new in this neighborhood will ever say that Myrna Kenton shirked her duty to roll out the welcome mat." Even if she had to roll it out right over the wishes of her newest neighbors.

I was only mildly curious about the mortal boy standing in my living room. Until Mrs. Kenton waved her arm like a circus ringmaster and said grandly, "I want to introduce my son, Angelo. He's known around the neighborhood as the one to go to when you want your yard work done well."

"That's great." Mom smiled warmly at him. She approves of people who work hard, even if they're cute teenage boys who may distract her daughter, who has just been told to leave the mortal stuff behind her. "This is my daughter, Prudence."

Angelo looked at me and smiled. "Hello, Prudence. That's a cool name."

And the world stopped. I mean it. Despite the fact that no one in his right mind would think Prudence was a cool name, Angelo's attention had turned on me like a hot spotlight on a stand-up comedian. Tag, I'm it. And it feels good.

Angelo was tall. Over six feet for sure, although I'm not great about judging height. He shaved. I could see the faint blue-black stubble on his jaw. I guessed he was probably a junior or senior at least. Lots of words came to mind the first time I saw Angelo. Forget "cute." That word was so not up to the task of describing him. Try "hot." "Scorching." "Sizzling." I wanted to see if the rest of him lived up to the first impression.

And yes, I was playing with fire. So sue me.

I aimed my best cheerworthy smile at Angelo, even though I knew mortals were pretty much not a good idea at the moment. "How long have you lived in Salem?"

He focused his blue eyes on me. "Oh, my mom's side of the family came over on the *Mayflower*. So I guess that means I've been here forever."

Suddenly I didn't care about the new rules. That boy could smile. It was like a beacon and all I wanted to do was spend a little quality time with a mortal very appropriately named Angelo.

I've had crushes before. I knew crushes come on hard and strong, like the rush of a cheering crowd when the football quarterback runs twenty yards for an unexpected touchdown. But when I looked at Angelo, *wow!* I'd never ever felt a crush come on like that. For a second I forgot to breathe. And I definitely forgot all about the witch/mortal thing that everyone kept warning me about.

About the Author

Kelly McClymer was born in South Carolina, but crossed the Mason-Dixon Line to live in Delaware at age six. After one short stint living in South Carolina during junior high, she has remained above the Line, and now lives in Maine with her husband and three children.

Writing has been Kelly's passion since her sixth-grade essay on how not to bake bread earned her an A+. After cleaning up the bread dough that oozed onto the floor, she gave up bread making for good and turned to writing as a creative outlet. A graduate of the University of Delaware (English major, of course), she spends her days writing and teaching writing. Her most recent novel, *Getting to Third Date*, is part of the Simon Pulse Romantic Comedy line.